# Books You Might Like

- Extreme Taboo Novellas: Two Sinful and Forbidden Erotica Collection by Bianca Gormly

- Forbidden Carnal Relations: Two Sinful Taboo Novellas for Adults by Ella Dowd

Sonya Link

# *Erotica: Extreme Taboo Stories*

Two Dirty, Naughty, Filthy, Sinful & Erotic Novella Collection for Adults

All Rights Reserved. No part of this publication may be reproduced in any form or by any means, including scanning, photocopying, or otherwise without prior written permission of the copyright holder. Copyright © 2022

This book is entirely a work of fiction. The names, characters and incidents portrayed in it are the work of the author's imagination. Any resemblance to actual persons, living or dead, events or localities is entirely coincidental.

**TABLE OF CONTENTS**

BOOKS YOU MIGHT LIKE ........................................................................ 1

STORY 01 ............................................................................................... 5

    CHAPTER 01 ..................................................................................... 6
    CHAPTER 02 ................................................................................... 18
    CHAPTER 03 ................................................................................... 38

STORY 02 ............................................................................................. 64

    CHAPTER 01 ................................................................................... 65
    CHAPTER 02 ................................................................................... 76
    CHAPTER 03 ................................................................................... 84
    CHAPTER 04 ................................................................................... 91
    CHAPTER 05 ................................................................................. 103

# Story 01

# Chapter 01

Matt had recently graduated from high school after turning 18 and was spending his summer off just being lazy. Sure, he worked out a few times a week and hung out with his friends when he could, but when they go together, they didn't do much because they all had the same idea to just relax for as long as they could until they all had to go off to school again in the fall. The friends he had with jobs were even lazier when they had time off, so it worked out well for all of them when the decision was to just be lazy and hang around in one of their rec-rooms. It was usually over at Matt's house, though. His mother Julie, older sister Jennifer, and even older sister Sally were all attractive in their own ways. Everyone wanted to get a peek at them as often as possible, including Matt.

39-year-old Julie was of average height and a little less than average weight. She had the wide hips and large 36C breasts of a woman who had mothered three children, but she had the stomach and butt of a teen. Her breasts, although large, were also still quite taught. She had her children young, right out of high school. (She conceived Sally in a maintenance closet during an assembly and birthed her a week after graduation at the tender age of 17), and did her best to stay in shape for her husband, even if he wasn't always around. Steve had always been a hard worker, but when he was home, he knew how to take care of his woman and had always treated her right. He never cheated on his wife and had given her the best sex of her life, year after year.

Sally, the oldest of the children at 22 years old, was a little short and had a body similar to her mothers, only without having had children yet. She was more athletic than the other women in her family, which made her legs were a little thick, and her waist wasn't as slim as it could be, but her skin was tight, her breasts were large at 36D, and she got as many looks as any woman could hope for. She worked at a bank, so she didn't work long days and got home quite early most afternoons. She spent most of her time working out between her getting out of work and her friends getting out of work.

At 20 years old, Jennifer was the best looking of the bunch. She was tall, slender, with a set of full 34B breasts on her chest that were almost but not quite a C cup, and an ass that wouldn't quit.

She looked more like the women on her father's side of the family than her sisters did, which was the model type. Two of her aunts were prominent models in the catalog scene, and Jennifer was planning on joining them after graduating college in another year. She was very popular on campus with both the students and faculty. And would be missed by everyone when she leaves.

As Matt lounged around the house all day, he felt like his sisters were constantly teasing him about something or another. It didn't bother him so much because they were always nice and non-malicious about it, but some of the time, the teasing just seemed a little off. It also seemed like they were wearing a lot less clothing around the house the last year or two. The touching had also increased. It was just harmless little touches of the hand or the leg, but they seemed to linger just a little too long or be just a little too close to his private areas. He knew it couldn't be true, but sometimes it seemed like they were coming on to him. The other night he had made a lude and sexist comment about what he wanted to do to some actress on the TV, which he thought would get an argument from his sisters, but instead, Jennifer just slapped him on the ass in passing on her way to the kitchen and called him a sexy beast. His mother was also acting strange around him. She would iron her blouse in just her bra or steal leisurely back to her room in just her underwear after throwing her work clothes into the laundry when she used to be so modest and composed around her children before.

"Maybe it's just the heat getting to all of us," Matt thought to himself as he went to bed one night after seeing Jen pull off her top with her back to her open door as he walked by her room. It had been especially hot that summer, to the point of being near-drought conditions. The sun had been beating down on them for weeks on end, and it was barely July. He was convinced that was the reason they were all acting so weird.

From that night on, Matt had troubled dreams. At first, it was just dreaming of him catching his sisters in various states of undress, but soon it deteriorated into full out sexual fantasies with both of them and his mother. Things weren't that much better during the daytime. He caught Sally on her way to her room in just a towel that wasn't actually hanging down past her butt. His mother started unbuttoning her blouse to iron it one morning but had neglected to wear a bra, nearly exposing both her breasts, but he only glimpsed one before she turned around and ironed facing away from him, still topless. And Jen was

constantly bouncing around the house in a thong and a tank top. She also seemed to be touching herself even more than she touched him, and that had escalated as well. She outright grabbed his crotch one night while sitting next to him on the couch, watching a movie. A bulge had developed in his pants during a sex scene, and she just reached over and grabbed it for a second to give it a good jostle before getting up to put her dessert bowl in the kitchen. Matt's dreams were that of a full out orgy that night.

When he awoke at 7:00 am the next Monday morning, Matt could hear the shower running as Sally prepared herself for work. He didn't get up right away, though. He just lay there on his bed, waiting until he couldn't stand to be in his room anymore. When he finally did get up an hour or so later, he threw on a T-shirt and boxer shorts before leaving his room. As he opened the door, he could hear Jen humming to herself as she brushed her teeth with the bathroom door open. He stopped in his tracks as he looked through the doorway at her with her back to him. She swayed her hips while brushing. He absentmindedly rubbed his member through his shorts when she bent over to spit and rinse her mouth out. She was only in a long and loose T-shirt herself, and he wasn't sure if she was wearing any panties underneath it. He got quite hard, staring at her like that. After she was done with her brushing and flossing, she began to brush her hair, and he was openly stroking himself through the thin layer of cotton, hiding his erection from the world.

"Are you just going to stare at me like that from the shadows all morning?" she asked after taking a few tentative brushes and glimpsing him in the mirror.

"I hadn't planned on it, no." he said as he continued rubbing himself openly.

"Well do something else. You're making me anxious standing there like a letch." She said as she went back to brushing her hair.

Matt just continued rubbing himself from over by his doorway, oblivious to everything but her. He was in a trance of sorts. All that he saw was her butt swaying under that shirt. All that he could think about was bending her over and sticking it to her. She leaned over a bit as she brushed, and the shirt bunched up a little at her waist. When she was finished brushing her hair, she started to scratch her eye up by the bridge of her nose, and then her shoulder as well with her other hand. She leaned down

even more, which pulled the hem of her shirt right up, and Matt realized right then that she wasn't wearing panties, and her butt was completely exposed to him. He himself absentmindedly took things another step further, pulled his dick out of his shorts, and stroked himself right there as he watched his sister in the bathroom.

"Matt? What are you doing?" She saw right away what had happened as she was watching for his reaction to her nakedness through the mirror. She was teasing him, but she didn't expect him to ever do that. "Put it away before someone sees us like this. Matt? Are you listening to me?" she whispered as she straightened up a little but didn't adjust her shirt. She had slipped up before when she had said he was making her anxious. She had meant to say "nervous." But the truth of the matter was that she was getting turned on by all of this playing around. She took a better look at his dick in the mirror, and while it wasn't the biggest in the world at 7", it was enough to make her heart race just that much faster, with thoughts of what it would be like to have him inside her as she gazed upon it.

Matt caught that lingering look and slowed down his strokes as he stepped toward her. Before either of them knew what they were doing or could even think of stopping it, Matt had a hold of Jen's hips and was slowly grinding himself up and down her naked and exposed crack, and she was enjoying it. She gasped every time he thrust himself up to her. As he thrust, he moved his hands up her sides until he felt the swell of her tits and gave them each a grope as he continued to push his member against her butt.

"Mom is gonna kill us if she sees this..." she moaned as she felt his strokes get longer and lower. His hands felt great up against her tits. He was just palming them, but the taboo of the situation was playing tricks with her mind and body. Her nipples felt hard, her center felt hot, and it was all that she could do to keep from crying out when his hands went back to her hips, and he thrust his dick up into her cunt. "Oh god..." she gasped as he slowly thrust into her again and again.

"Oh god... Oh god we have to be quiet... or mom will catch us for sure..." she cried almost silently and out of breath as she tried to hold in her screams. Her brother was poking her from behind. He bent her over the bathroom sink with the door open to anyone who should pass it. As he pushed her down farther, she grabbed the sides of the sink to support herself. She could feel his strong hands on her hips, pulling her back into him, and

she wished that they were back up on her tits, under her shirt, pinching her nipples.

Matt was in heaven as he pumped his dick into his sister's quim. He wasn't even thinking about her as he fucked her over the bathroom sink. He was only thinking about fucking, and how great it felt to be back inside a cunt again. He wasn't a virgin, but for some reason, he felt like he was doing something that he had never done before as he repeatedly jabbed at his sister's slick opening. He slid his hands up her bare flesh under her shirt as it hung away from her body and fulfilled her silent wish as he grabbed onto her tits again. This time it was skin against skin, and he used a little more finesse than last time as he pinched her nipples and leaned over her to kiss the side of her neck.

"Oh god this feels so good," she groaned as they fucked each other as best they could in this position. Caution was forgotten as everything they did grew louder the longer they continued. Their mother was blissfully asleep on the other side of the house, but Julie was the farthest thing from their minds as he rammed his dick as hard as he could. Their flesh slapped together audibly as his hips collided with her ass cheeks. With all of the sensations attacking her at once, Jen yelled out something Matt never expected to hear her say. "Pull my hair," she called out as she looked him in the eyes through the mirror. "Pull it Matt... Pull my hair..."

He did as he was told. He let go of her right tit, pulled his hand out from under her shirt, and grabbed her hair as he continued to thrust into her. His thrusts became more of a jerking motion, with slam after slam against her rump. He was bucking into her with all his might when he did something that neither of them saw coming. He let go of her other tit and smacked her ass with a loud "THWACK!" After jabbing her a few more times, he smacked her ass cheek again. "TWACK!" As they found their new rhythm, they picked up the pace, and so did his smacks. Every other thrust into each other, he smacked her ass again with another loud "THWACK!"

"Oh my god I love this..." she cried out loud as she fucked back into her brother. Her left ass cheek was feeling red and swollen, but it felt so good every time he laid his hand into her.

"THWACK!"

"More..." she called out to him.

"TWACK!"

"Oh god yes..."

"THWACK!"

"MORE!...," she cried again.

"TWACK! THWACK! TWACK!"

He was now hitting her every time as he stabbed her from behind with his cock. They were quickly approaching their orgasms, and Jen was more and more vocal about it. Their mother would be waking soon, and Jen's cries and screams and moans would be the cause of it. They didn't care. They were intent on finishing what they had started and to finished each other off.

"Oh yeah... oh yeah... oh yeah..." she cried as she reached her peak. "Ohh... FUCK! Shit! Oh..."

Matt let out a groan as well as he released his seed inside his sister's womb. They waited a few long moments as they gasped for air to fill their emptied lungs before separating. Jen pulled down her shirt as Matt pushed his dick back into his shorts.

"I think need another shower," she said as her brother started to exit the room. "It's a good thing I woke up early today, or I would be late for class. We'll have to do this again sometime, when I'm a little more prepared." With that, she turned on the shower and closed the door to her again, staring brother.

Matt went back into his room and changed his clothes so that the stink of sex on him wouldn't be so powerful. After loading himself up with deodorant, he went down to the kitchen to make himself some breakfast. He saw his mom standing over by the fridge with her robe hanging wide open, so he went to the cabinet to get himself some cereal. When he opened the cabinet, he heard his mother jump and yelp in surprise, which caused him to jump as well. When he looked at his mother, he caught just a glimpse of both breasts as she pulled her robe mostly closed, but leaving one breast still mostly showing. He also noticed that she wasn't wearing panties as his mother pushed the material against her skin to make sure nothing was showing.

"I'm sorry Matt, I didn't hear you come down." She said she continued to compose herself and finally covered up her other boob.

"Sorry I scared you, Mom." He said with a smile as he moved over toward the fridge. He felt her crotch brush up against his own as the two passed, switching places with each other.

"Did you hear your sister screaming this morning? It sounded like she broke her leg." Julie said as she sipped her coffee.

Matt nearly fell over when he heard her ask that. His legs went to jelly, and his gut tensed up and nearly hurled. If he had eaten, he might have. But he was looking in the fridge at the time and just simply went with the story his mother already made up. "Yeah, I did. Why do you think I'm awake so early during my vacation? She must have stubbed her toe." He let out a sigh of relief when his mother appeared to buy his story. Later in the morning, when Jen finally came down on her way out to school, she validated his story by saying she stubbed her toe, without even checking with him first.

The next few days went by fairly normally, all things considered. Matt and Jen were constantly touching each other, but nothing all that serious really happened between them. Someone was always around the house to keep the two from going further. They would make out, grope, and masturbate each other a little when they were alone, just to get them turned on, but neither of them ever got to finish the job. When they were out in the public areas of the house, they would cool it a little, but there would still be the ass-slaps and the light stroking of one body part or another incognito.

On Thursday morning, Matt woke up to what he thought would be a change in routine from all of the playing it safe that they were doing. He could feel a mouth around his dick, sucking him as hard as it had ever been sucked. When his eyes opened, he looked down towards his lap, were all he could see was his sister's eyes staring right back into his own. It felt wonderful to wake up to a blowjob like this. He had been sucked off, but he had never had anyone there when he woke up like this before.

He motioned for Jen to turn around but to continue sucking him as she was. When she got her legs up by his head, he spread her knees apart and slipped two fingers into her already moist cavity, which made her scream into his dick, which thankfully muffled it. As she bobbed her head on his cock, he pushed his fingers in her tunnel at the same pace. The faster she bobbed her head, the faster he fingered her. She started to moan and groan around his member, and the vibrations were driving him wild. As amazing as that was, her tongue was pushing him over the edge. It was all over the place as it swirled around his head and shaft.

Matt ducked his head between her legs and stuck his tongue into her folds as his fingers held her lips open. He licked all

around her pussy and probed around for her G-spot now. He thought he saw his bedroom door move out of the corner of his eye, but it was still closed like it was before, so he didn't let that slow him down much. He went right back to licking around her opening, trying to suck up every bit of nectar to come out of her, eliciting louder and more enthusiastic moans out of his sister as he went along. When he moved his mouth onto her clit and started sucking it, her moans turned to screams around his cock, which triggered his orgasm. He shot his load down her mouth, and she swallowed as much of it as she could. He was cumming so hard he had to pause for a moment before he could go on. As he let off of her clit he heard some movement downstairs and groaned as he fell back onto his pillow.

"Sounds like Mom is up." He said as Jen licked up the last of his ejaculate from her face and lips. "You had better take a shower too. Did you cum at all?"

"I sure as hell did. Twice," she sighed as she crawled up his body. "I was building to an orgasm, fingering myself when you woke up. You slipped your fingers into me and it was all over." She straddled his lower body and ground her slit down onto his softening member as she leaned down to kiss his lips. He knew he had just cum in her mouth, but that didn't matter. What they were doing was already so taboo. Something like that was hardly in his mind after 69ing with his sister. He kissed her back and loved every second of it.

"You has better stop that, Jenny," he groaned as he broke the kiss. "Mom is up downstairs, and you're a screamer. Go take a shower."

He grabbed her hips and helped her up off of his lap and sitting next to him as he got up out of bed. She did as he suggested and showered as he went down and started what was to be a normal day of teasing from all of his female family members from then on out. His mother was ironing in just a slip and panties when he went for breakfast. When sally got home from work, she stripped off her blouse as she ran up the stairs giving him a great view of her knockers confined in a lacy white bra. Later that night, he made out a little with Jen in her room, but they didn't go any farther.

Their next chance for some real action came on Saturday night, though. Sally was out with friends, and Steve was taking Julie out for dinner and dancing to celebrate being home from another long business trip. The moment their parents were out, the two of them were tickling each other and chasing around

the house. Jen decided that now was as good a time as any to play hard to get, and Matt went along with it because it was a nice bit of fun having to work for his prize. When Matt finally did catch up to her, they were in the powder room over by the kitchen. He pinned her up against the sink by his hips, with him holding her arms folded against her chest.

"Remember this position?" he whispered into her ear as he held her squirming body. "This is how we first met."

He emphasized "met" with a pelvic thrust up against her ass through their jeans. He rubbed up against her a few times like this before she turned and kissed him. Letting go of her arms, he moved his hands down her torso, over her mounds on her jeans. And then up under her tight t-shirt. He mauled her breasts over her bra barbarically for a few moments before pulling it down and giving her nipples a good tweak, his hips still pressing her hard up against the sink with long and slow thrusts. She fumbled to undo her jeans and pushed them down with her thong as far as she could while being pinned in the way she was. Matt let go of her tits for just a moment to do the same with his jeans. After slipping his pants down enough to expose himself, he pushed hers down just a little farther and returned his hands to her mammaries as he thrust up against her crack, flesh on flesh this time.

"Oh god Matt, that feels so good..." she cooed as he pulled her nipples out as far as they would go. "Fuck me damn it... Just fuck me..." Not one to ignore such a fun request, he bent his knees a little more and pushed the head of his cock up into her dripping hole. "Yeah, bro... Fuck me! Fuck me hard..."

He did just that. Right away, he started pounding her as hard as he could. He drove his cock into her against and again with powerful and rapid strokes. She felt like he was using a heated dildo attached to a jackhammer on her twat. His hips were slapping up against her ass so hard and fast. She immediately needed to brace her hands up against the wall behind the sink to hold herself up to his vaginal assault.

"Oh yeah... Fuck that's so good..." She cried out, just taking what he was giving her without adding much back to the experience yet. "Fuck! Matt... that's so fucking good..."

"You like that... don't you, Jen... You like the way... your little brother... pounds your pussy... You like the way I stick it to you..." he said to her as he grabbed her hair without her asking this time. He just figured it was something that she liked. "Make

me run... and chase you... To give you what you wanted anyway... You're a bad girl Jenny... You need to be punished..."

"Oh yeah Matt... I've been baaaad... Spank me Matt... Spank me while you fuck me..." she was shoving her ass back at him now, trying to get his cock deeper with each thrust.

"THWACK!" He smacked the side of her ass hard.

"Oh yeah Matt... Spank me..."

"THWACK!"

"Punish me for teasing you... Spank me for running from you..." she cried, out of breath and sweating now.

He spanked the left ass cheek a couple more times, and then he did what he should have done earlier in the week. He switched hands and spanked her right cheek while pulling her hair with his left hand, all the while they fucked into each other with reckless abandon. After a minute or two of this, his hands started to hurt nearly as much as her ass cheeks. And so he decided to cool them off by groping her soft cool tits again. He eventually grew tired of this position, though, as much as he loved it. He pulled her up by her breasts and turned her around. He pressed her back up against the wall as he entered her face to face and kissed her.

"Oh yeah..." she cooed with a pleased tone in her voice. "Do me slow like this Matt... A slow screw against the wall..."

This position was giving both of them a chance to catch their breath, as well as holding off Matt's orgasm, which had been rapidly approaching before he paused to turn them around. Jen didn't really care which way she was facing or which way he came at her. She loved the taboo of having his cock in her. It was almost as much as she loved him as a brother for all the years before they started having sex. But this wasn't love right now. This was raw animal lust, and she was getting the most out of it. She already cum several times while bent over the sink, and he was preparing her for another one here against the wall.

"Fuck, Jenny... Your pussy feels so good... So wet and so tight..." he said in a hushed voice as he continued his slow and steady strokes. "Your little brother loves your tight and wet hole..."

"Bro... There is nothing little about you... and you can fuck me all day... any time you want to..." she said to him before kissing him again.

They stayed like that for another few minutes, just slowly grinding themselves against each other up against the wall for another few minutes before the urge to go faster again overcame them. She motioned for him to lay down on the floor, where she quickly followed him and straddled his cock like she had the other day.

"We never did finish this the other morning, did we?" she said with a smile as she grabbed his rod gently, stroked him a couple of times, and eased herself down on him.

"No, we didn't. This is about where we left off," he said. Well-rested and ready for me, he wanted his sister's body more than ever.

"Fuck, bro, I love the way you fill me up..." She shifted around on his cock for a few moments before pulling up off his cock. So as little of him was inside her without actually letting him pop out. "Your cock feels so good, I just want to plunge it into me again and again." She sank back down on him, which elicited a groan from both of them. "I'm going to fuck you like this until you cum, Matt. I want you to cum inside me Matt. I want you to fill me up like you did last week."

She pulled up off of him again and slammed herself down a little faster than before. She repeated this a few more times, gaining speed each time she dropped herself on his cock until he started to thrust back up at her until they were fucking each other. They built up their rhythm to a maddening pace of hot and wild fucking before Matt couldn't take it anymore. When he announced to his sister that he was going to come, she started fucking him even faster than before until she finally felt him squirt inside her. She then slowed down but kept fucking him until he started to soften up, and she felt him fall out of her.

"That was the best fuck ever Bro. You are the best fuck ever." She said as she lay down on top of him on the powder room floor, with their legs out in the hallway. "I thought that first time was as good as it gets, but you proved me wrong Matt. You proved me so wrong."

They kissed and made out until they regained their strength, and then they grabbed their clothes, got dressed, and watched TV until their parents got home. They thought they had themselves a wonderful and private fuck session in their big empty house. What they didn't know was that their oldest sister Sally had come home to grab a change of clothes for her night out and that she not only heard but saw her two younger siblings going at it in the powder room by the kitchen. She didn't

catch the whole thing. She came in as he was spanking her and had to shortly leave after he pressed her up against the wall, but Sally could see from what little she was there for to know what was going on in the house, and that deep down inside she wanted some too.

## Chapter 02

The next few weeks for Matt went pretty much the way that the first one did after having sex with Jen, the younger of his two older sisters. The two of them went on fooling around for the most part, and only having sex when they thought they had the house to themselves, like when their father and sister were at work, and their mother was shopping, or out jogging in the afternoon between lunch and dinner. What they never seemed to realize was that their older sister Sally had caught them during their second sex session and had been secretly keeping her eye on them as well, wishing that she could join in. Her only problem was that she wasn't as outgoing as the other members of her family. She was actually quite shy, unlike everyone else who seemed to have a well of courage as deep as the ocean.

While Sally was spying from the shadows, their mother, Julie, was noticing changes in them as well. She noticed that their playing around became a lot more familiar and physical. She also noticed that they were spending a lot more time together and in each other's rooms a lot more than they ever had been before, even when they were young. Her husband was oblivious when she asked him, but she knew that something was up, even though she couldn't quite place a finger on what was actually going on between her younger two children.

Though Julie was in the dark about what was going on, she wasn't far behind her daughter Jennifer in her lust for Matt. When his body had grown to its current shape, she found herself getting slightly excited when she would see him walk around in boxer shorts on the weekends, and she got downright wet when she noticed a sizable bulge in his pants from time to time. After a time, her guilt at her feelings went away, and she started doing all that she could to encourage him to grow hard around the house. When he was growing up, she was a very proper mother who was always fully dressed and not wearing anything too revealing. Lately, though, she had been hardly wearing anything around her son at times. She would make sure to tease him just a little bit more each time she would see him. At first, it was just a few buttons undone on her blouses, but after time it became removing blouses to iron them in front of him while he ate breakfast or running around in a half-closed robe. The other day she had the lower half of her robe so open

that if he chose to look, he could have seen her pussy as she passed him.

Matt was looking. He saw that, as well as every other bit of flesh that she had decided to show him. He had suspicions that the flashes were intentional for a while now, but he had no idea what to do about it. He figured that his affair with Jennifer had been a fluke. Once he had realized what he had done, he was surprised that she hadn't called the cops on him and gotten him kicked out of the house. He was glad that things had worked out as well as they had, but he wasn't sure that things would go as smoothly with his mother, and he didn't dare push the line any further than she was willing to set it beforehand.

One morning, after fooling around with his sister before breakfast, Matt found out just how far things could go with his mother. The two children had been groping each other up in his room until they heard Julie banging some pans and dishes around in the kitchen. Jennifer went to take a shower before going out with her friends while Matt decided to just show up for breakfast as is, in a pair of boxer shorts and a t-shirt. He wasn't worried about his erection tenting his shorts, as he was almost sure by now that his mother was showing off for him.

When he arrived down in the kitchen, he found his mother by the stove in a slightly darker than skin tone blouse with a nice floral pattern on it and a slightly darker loose and flowing skirt hanging from her hips to her knees. It wasn't until he got closer that he noticed it was flesh-colored for a reason. It was practically see-through. The flowers that seemed scattered randomly around the back and sides were strategically placed on the front to camouflage but not entirely hide her nipples. The skirt, upon closer inspection, proved to be almost but not quite as see-through as the blouse; it was a slightly darker tone. Matt couldn't make out any details, but he could also tell that his mother wasn't wearing any underwear. He could also see quite clearly that she was shaved down below (he had known for a while, as she had flashed herself to him many times by now, but it was still a nice sight). Otherwise, the skirt would have shown quite obviously any bush had she chosen to grow it out. She looked hot, and Matt couldn't believe she was so brazen about her sexuality.

"Good morning, Mom." Matt said as he reached up to the cabinet above the stove for a coffee cup.

He could have gone to any number of other places for any number of cups, they were all over the place with five coffee

drinkers in the house, but he didn't. He chose that particular cabinet to judge her reaction when he glanced his boner up against her barely covered ass. He expected her to just continue frying up the sausages and pancakes, but she did what he had always dreamed she would do, but least expected of her. She pushed herself back up against him firmly.

"Good morning, honey. You've been Up and Able quite early a lot lately." She returned, emphasizing "up" and "able" while glancing just so quickly down to his crotch for a split second, and then smiling as she dished out the goods from the stove. "Would you like to have breakfast with me?"

"I'd love to Mom." He said as he took his coffee to a seat at the table, with her right behind with plates and forks.

Just after he sat down, she followed suit and sat in the same chair right in his lap, pressing her back into him, practically spooning him as they sat at the table, his erection planted square between the cheeks of her ass, and no denying the motives behind it. She placed the plates and forks on the table, then hugged her son tightly from the side as she turned to him and kissed him on the cheek. She was trying to make a move on him and desperately wanted to kiss his lips, but she just couldn't bring herself to do it.

"I love you Matt," she said with a wide-eyed smile, still struggling to hold herself back from devouring her son.

"Me too Mom," said Matt. He saw the look of lust in her eyes and was tempted himself to lean forward and suck her into him. But just before he could make both of their wishes come true, she quickly stood up as they heard Jennifer start the shower upstairs. "Would you like a glass of milk with that?" she asked as she walked into the kitchen again.

"That sounds great, Mom," he replied as he grabbed a fork and started eating his breakfast.

They both ate in silence, each trying to figure out where this would all go from here and stealing furtive glances at each other. Julie couldn't believe that she had been so careless to forget that her younger daughter was still in the house. She needed to change to keep Jennifer from seeing her as some kind of cheap whore. She waited until she was finished eating before quickly clearing her plate to the sink and went into her room to change into something more fitting for a mother to wear but still enticing to a teenage boy.

When Matt was finished eating, he too cleared his place and went to change into something for his basketball game with friends later in the morning. As he rounded the corner at the top of the stairs, he saw Jennifer through the bathroom door, which was open just enough to give him a peek at her as she brushed her hair naked. He pushed the door open wide as he watched her with a grin on his face.

"Little miss naked sis isn't afraid Mom is going to catch her with the door open like that?" he asked as he stepped into the room and hugged her from behind, and pressed his bulging shorts into her rear.

"Look who's talking? Aren't you the one who fucked me from behind with that very same door wide open, while Mom was sleeping just a couple feet away downstairs?" she replied as she pressed back against him. She loved the feel of his cock between her cheeks and wished that he wasn't wearing his shorts so that he could fuck her where she stood.

"Why yes I am. Wanna try it with her awake this time? We just ate breakfast together." He said, moving her hair out of the way and kissing her on the shoulder.

"You're kidding! She's up this early? And you still want to do it?" she gasped. The idea excited her beyond belief.

"Well we might have to gag you to keep her from hearing us, but that could be fun to do sometime anyway." He smoothly said as he pressed tighter into her ass, grinding his covered cock into her soft posterior.

"And the spanking? You don't think she would get just a little suspicious hearing you slapping the hell out of her daughter's ass?" she asked, reaching back to push his shorts down and revealing his cock to the fresh air. He backed away for a moment to step out of them and then picked them up before rubbing his naked cock up against her bare ass. He knew she was already talked into having sex with him. All that he had to do now was take her.

"Maybe I should just tie you up?" he suggested as he slid the shorts up her side and then showed them to her. "Here, suck on these. They're clean."

She did as he requested and let him stuff his shorts into her mouth, but she was reeling from a bolt of electricity that shot through her when he said he should tie her up. She had thought about being tied up before but had never dared ask anyone to try it on her ever. She didn't trust any of her boyfriends that

much up to this point. But this was her brother, who she could trust with her body, mind, and soul. He would never do anything to physically endanger her, and if he wanted to tie her up while he fucked her senseless, she was going to let him do it!

Matt had been thinking of tying her up for a week or so now. But the idea of bondage had been in his head for months, and he even asked a couple of his girlfriends from school if they would let him. The answer was always no, but the gleam in his sister's eye told him that he might finally hear a yes, and have a subject that would be willing to go along with his perversions. It wouldn't be today, but soon he would tie his pretty sister up and have his way with her.

For now, Matt was content to just bend her over the bathroom sink for the third time in a month. He grabbed her hips and looked her in the eye through the mirror. He eased his cock into her from behind. She woke up excited every morning. The thought of playing around sexually with her younger brother, and they had been fooling around just before she took her shower. She was wet enough already that he didn't have any trouble pushing into her in one long, slow, agonizing stroke.

Jennifer whimpered at how he was taking his time to plug her hole. She liked her sex hard and fast, and the pace he was taking was torturous to her. He took his time pushing into her, and he seemed to take even more time pulling out. She could feel every bump and ridge on his cock as it slid across the walls of her vagina. It was torture, it was driving her insane, and she was about to explode with an orgasm after only five or six strokes!

Matt grabbed his sister's tits and felt their weight before adjusting his grip and pinched her nipples. They were so stiff and erect that they felt like pencil erasers between his fingers and thumb. Once he pulled them out, he noticed that her entire body was convulsing in what must have been an Earth-shattering orgasm. Her knees trembled, her head thrown back, and her eyes closed, and even though she was braced up against the sink, he had to hold her up to keep her from falling to the floor, but he never stopped slowly pumping himself in her pussy.

She was on the edge of insanity. All that she could feel was her brother's cock sliding in and out of her cunt, and his hands palming her breasts and pulling her nipples. The rest of the world had disappeared from her as she writhed in orgasmic bliss. As her focus started to return to her, she opened her eyes and looked into Matt's through the mirror. As they locked onto

each other, he picked up the pace a little, and she felt it start all over again. She cried out through the shorts in her mouth when he pulled her hair back and kissed her neck. She was headed for another orgasm, and she was getting there faster than she ever had before.

Matt could see the pleasure on his sister's face. Even with his shorts stuck in her mouth. They weren't muting the cries of her second orgasm in as many minutes as efficiently as he had hoped they would, but with any luck, their mother still wouldn't hear them fucking in the upstairs bathroom. After what they shared at breakfast, he wasn't expecting her to be up here while Jenny was still in the house. His mother seemed to be making a move on him, but there was no way she could be dumb enough to attempt it with her daughter so close by, could she? At least downstairs, there were other rooms to duck away to, but up here, there isn't much room to move; maybe that's why screwing his sister in the bathroom with the door open and his shorts in her mouth was so exciting? He was fairly certain that there was no chance of their mother coming up here this early in the day, but if she did, then they would surely be caught with no escape.

No such thoughts were entering Jen's mind, however. She came twice with her brother pumping her hole as slowly as he could, and now that he was finally giving it to her at a good and steady clip, she was headed for a third. She was proud of Matt for his control and endurance. Most other men that she had been with, if not all of them, would have just shoved themselves into her as fast as possible and blown their wad the moment that her pussy clamped down on their dicks, but not her brother. He started out slow and got faster from there, and even though she was coming for the third time.

She passed out from being fucked so well and never finished that last thought. Matt was able to ease her down to the floor without much fuss and keep the noise to a minimum. If he had let her drop, the noise would be sure to arouse the suspicions of their mother, and he just couldn't let that happen. He pulled her wet hair out of her face and patted her forehead to try to rouse her in a soothing manner, which he was thankful appeared to be working. He didn't exactly know what to do with a fainting victim and was just happy to see that she was going to pull through this.

"What happened?" she asked with a glazed look on her face.

"You came so hard you fainted," he said as he brushed his knuckles over her cheek. "I was worried there for a moment."

"The way you fuck me, I don't think I'd mind if I died with you in my pussy," she nearly whispered as she looked up into his eyes from the floor. She reached out for something to hoist herself up, but all that she could find was her brother's stiff prick jutting out from his groin. "Unconscious girls turn you on there, Matt? Are you one of those guys who likes to take advantage of the first girl to pass out at a party? How many times have you done me in my sleep, Matt? Are you doing the rest of the family like that too? Even Dad?"

"Actually, I never finished. You passed out before I could." He responded, helping her sit up. "And I would never do anything gay with Dad. There isn't anything attractive about men."

"Maybe not for you, but I love a nice hard cock to suck on. Now give it here and I'll have that swelling down in a jiff. I'll even suck all the bad stuff out for you," she said as she tugged him closer and leaned down to suck his dick into her mouth. She sucked in as much as she could as fast as she could before coming up again. "I just love the way you taste after being in me."

After that last comment, she went back to sucking him off as fast as she could. She gobbled him down and sucked as she let him back out. She swiveled her hand back and forth as she stroked him up and down along with her vacuuming mouth. His sister worked his cock for all that she was worth, slobbering all over it in an attempt to get him off and get him out of the bathroom so that she could finish getting ready for her day. She loved and needed the fuck that he had just given her, and she really enjoyed sucking his cock, but after the slow fuck he had just given her, she felt the need to do this fast. She looked like a porn star the way she bobbed her head up and down his shaft. Matt leaned back against the wall. Even though he was breaking a sweat just from the feelings running through his shaft, he was in heaven with his sister going hog-wild on his cock. She felt like she was going to suck his brains out through his dick or that he would simply turn inside out. She paused, her head bobbing for just a moment, and her tongue went mad on his cock head. This was too much for her younger brother, and he uncontrollably spewed into her mouth without warning her. He didn't have any warning himself. He was breathless one moment and cumming in her mouth the next. She didn't seem to mind at all that he came without warning her and just continued sucking on him as hard as she could, swallowing every drop until she milked him dry.

After unexpectedly sucking every drop out of her younger brother, Jennifer got up off of the floor, wrapped a towel around her, and said to Matt, "You worked up quite a sweat just now. You should take a shower before you go back downstairs." And with that, she left the bathroom and closed the door behind her.

Matt just sat there on the floor for a few minutes until he could move his legs again, and as soon as he had enough strength to pick himself back up, he took his sister's advice and jumped into the shower to wash the sweat from their encounter off of his body. When he went for a towel to dry himself off, he noticed that he hadn't planned this impromptu shower ahead of time and had neglected to bring one into the bathroom with him. He really didn't feel like donning his sleeping attire again, so he decided to make the quick trip to his room naked. Since the only person he expected to see was his sister, who had just sucked him off, and was unlikely to bust him for being naked in the hallway, he thought it would be the best solution to his problem.

When he reached his room, he quickly wished that he had put something on, as what he found was his mother kneeling on the floor, picking up his dirty laundry from around the room. She was leaning over away from him, showing off her ass in a white pair of short shorts as she reached under his bed. He could see the whale tail of her blue thong peaking out of them. When she moved around, he could see that she was also wearing a light blue baby-t, and her big tits were hanging down and wobbling around bra-less as she picked up his clothes. For just a quick moment, he thought about going back to the bathroom and waiting for her to go downstairs, but after thinking about the way she was acting at breakfast, he decided to give her a show and see what her reaction would be to her naked son.

"Hey, Mom," he casually said as he waltzed into the room as naked as he could be. He walked over to his bed where he still had a basket of clean laundry, grabbed a towel, and dried himself facing his starstruck mother. After tossing it back onto the bed, he started rooting through the basket for a pair of boxer shorts. He ignored his mother's gaze, acting like it was no big deal that he was naked in front of her, but saw enough to know that she was staring at him and had paused her search for dirty clothes just to watch him. He spotted a pair of shorts in the basket, but he also knew that his mother couldn't see them from where she was and decided to ignore them for the moment and continue his exposure for as long as he could. He

instead walked over to his dresser and looked in there for something to wear. Finding that he really didn't have anything in there, he turned and gave his mother a goofy smile.

"I guess I'm going commando today," he said as he walked back over to the basket. He was getting hard from showing off to his mother, and there was no way that she could miss it. He was on full display for her as he moved back across the room and went into the basket again, this time for a pair of khaki shorts. "Oh, here's a pair of boxers," he said as he "found" them, not really wanting to go commando today. He turned towards Julie to give his mother one last look at him as he slipped his shorts up and stroked his meat a couple of times before he stuffed his mostly hard penis into them. After giving them one last adjustment, grabbing himself and pulling the leg of the shorts tight against his dick, looking his mother right in the eyes, he noticed that she was only focused on his crotch and oblivious to the rest of the world. "I have a basketball game with the guys before it gets too hot out. I'll see you later Mom." And with that, he was off. He left the room, and his mother practically drooling over her son's tool.

Julie finally shook herself out of her trance but neglected to pick anything else up off of her son's floor. She was still in shock at what her son had just shone on her. She nearly bumped into her daughter as they both headed for the stairs. She freaked out as she was completely shaken from her daydreams of Matt stroking himself in front of her like some kind of porn star, and Jennifer actually had to grab her mother's arm to keep her from falling down the stairs as she crashed back into reality.

"Are you ok Mom? You look like you just saw a ghost." Jennifer said as she walked down the stairs in front of her mother.

For some unknown reason to her, Julie decided to go the honest route and tell her daughter the truth. "Do you know what your brother just did? I was in his room picking up his dirty laundry to finish up this load so that I could wash some stuff that I want to wear tomorrow when he walked in stark naked, with a semi-hard penis, and walked around like that until he put on a pair of shorts and left. The nerve of that boy!" Julie neglected that she had gone into his room while he was in the shower and waited for him to return so that she could catch a glimpse of him before he dressed. She also left out the part about him stroking himself, knowing that would only disturb Jennifer, and not wanting to upset her like that.

"Wow!" Jen was shocked at her mother's confession. "Really? What did you do? What did you say to him?"

"I didn't say anything to him. It was over before I could get a handle on the situation. Once he left the room I picked up my basket and bumped into you." She said as she hefted the basket up a bit to emphasize her statement.

"Wow. You should give him a good lecture for that. Where is he now?"

"He's not here. He said he had a ballgame with his friends before it gets hot out. It'll have to wait until he gets back," she said as she headed into the laundry room.

"Can you wait until I'm back home before you do it? I want to hear that." Asked Jennifer as her mother started loading the clothing into the washing machine.

"No Jenny. I wouldn't do that to you, and I won't do that to your brother. I'll have a talk with him in private as soon as he gets back. We can't have him acting like this house is a barn."

"No, that would be uncouth."

"Such big words! You've been studying!" said Julie as she finished placing the clothes into the washing machine. "I'm so proud of you!" she playfully cried as she hugged her daughter to her, immediately feeling Jennifer's hard nipples poking into her own surprisingly hard nipples. She quickly broke the hug, hoping that her daughter hadn't noticed her arousal too. "So where are you off to so early today, Jen?"

"Oh, there's a sale today that my friends and I are hitting up. The store opens at ten, so we are getting there when it opens to beat some of the rush."

"Shouldn't you get there early to beat the rush?"

"Hell no!" Jennifer called out with authority. "We don't want to get trampled. We just want a good deal on some dresses. The store had plenty of everything last night when we checked it out. Even if there are a hundred crazy screaming women in front of us we'll still get a good deal on a decent selection."

"Well I wish you luck in your search. When will you be back?"

"Oh, I won't be back until after dinner. We still have the normal things to do after we leave the store you know," she said as she winked to her mother and walked out the door to her car.

Julie spent the rest of the day straightening up the house, subconsciously waiting for her son to return, hoping that he would be hard, and at least as daring as he was earlier in his room. After washing the dishes and dusting the shelves, all that she could think about was the way her son looked naked in his room that morning. It had only been an hour since she had nearly creamed herself in front of him, and she was already creaming herself again. She dropped the feather duster on the coffee table and sat on the couch to watch some TV and calm herself. After flipping through the channels a few times, she decided that there wasn't anything on, and she was still moistening between her legs.

She absentmindedly started rubbing herself through her shorts with her left hand as she flipped blindly through the channels with her right. She stopped on an exercise program and just stared at the host's pectoral muscles. He was a young guy in his late twenties, and he was fit. He looked a lot like her son when she thought about it. The more she thought about it, the more she thought about her son's body, the more she thought about his cock, the more she rubbed herself closer and closer to orgasm. She dropped the remote and used her free hand to grab her left tit through her shirt and groped it as hard as she could.

Rubbing herself over her shorts wasn't doing it for her, though. She slipped her hand under the waistband and into her panties and started rubbing her fingers directly into her mound. But this was still too confining for her needs. She let go of her breast, pulled her other from her shorts, and undid her fly before pushing her shorts down to her ankles. She rubs both of her hands into her pussy. She rubbed and prodded at her pussy lips until she couldn't take it anymore and slipped the middle finger of her right hand into her steaming cunt.

She didn't even see the TV anymore as she pulled her labia open with one hand and pushed the rest of the fingers of her other hand into her twat. All she could see was the image of her son standing in front of her with his semi-hard cock right at her face level up in his room. She wanted to reach out and grab him so bad when it was happening, she wanted to replace his hand with her own when he stroked himself, but she had resisted. She had always been faithful to her husband. She hadn't even been tempted by another man until now. It wasn't until she saw her son get home from school all sweaty one day a year or two ago that she started having straying thoughts, and they were all about her son. She wanted him so bad that she was picturing

what it would have been like to reach out and grab his cock up in his room. She imagined leaning forward and sucking his cock head into her mouth and jerking him off until he came down her throat. She thought about him taking her and throwing her onto the bed or pounding his man meat into her flooded canal as she lay face down on the floor and making her cum screaming. She heard the back door open and knew it was her son. She pictured him finding her like this and crawling between her legs to fuck her on the couch. She was so close to cumming, but she just couldn't let that happen. She couldn't let him catch her like this.

Julie quickly pulled her shorts up while standing and finished zipping them just as Matt walked into the room. She was flush, her heavy breathing was causing her chest to rise and fall dramatically, and he saw her pull her hands quickly away from the waistband of her shorts and then cross them under her breasts, and then just as quickly drop them down to her sides again. He knew that she had been masturbating, just now in the living room, and she was trying to hide it. He pretended that he hadn't noticed and let her keep her dignity for a little longer.

"Hey Mom. I'm going to wash up real quick. What's for lunch?" he asked as he headed towards the stairs.

"Lunch? I hadn't really thought about lunch. I guess I could make up some sandwiches if you like?" She hoped he hadn't seen how flush her face was, and she tried to hide her ragged breath from him as she answered as calmly as she could.

"That would be great. I'll be back down in a minute."

Matt ran upstairs and into the bathroom. He deliberately didn't grab a towel for his shower this time, hoping that his mother would find another reason to be in his room when he got back out. He had a raging hard-on in the shower as he thought about what they would do together when he was done washing himself. He didn't play with himself, though. As much as he wanted to, he had to restrain himself and save it up for his hot-bodied mother.

She wasn't in his room when he got there, though. After he left her in the living room, she was shaking and went to the kitchen to make lunch as she calmed her nerves. She thought she had finally gotten herself under control when Matt showed up and sat at the table, but she was wrong. She grabbed the plate of sandwiches off the counter and carried it over to the kitchen table, and placed it in front of him. She grabbed one of them off the plate and sat across from him as he grabbed two and started eating. She didn't know it, but he could see a wet spot on her

shorts between her legs where she had pressed her shorts into herself as she prepared their meal.

Julie momentarily considered confronting her son about the incident up in his room that morning, but as soon as the thought crossed her mind, she started getting wet all over again. Her breasts started heaving as she ate, and she started pressing her legs together to try to squash the pressure between them. It wasn't working though, it only intensified the feelings, and as she finished eating, she started rubbing her thighs together, back and forth, stimulating herself as best as she could do without being spotted. All that she could think about was seducing her son. She looked at him through the glass table and could see the bulge in his shorts. He was hard again, and she wished that he were naked again. All of a sudden, confronting him about this morning didn't sound like such a bad idea.

"So, Matt, did you enjoy showing off your naked body to your mother in your room this morning?" she asked as he took the last bite of his sandwich, nearly choking when he heard her words.

Matt considered his possible answers thoroughly as he chewed that last bite and settled on what he would say as he swallowed. "Yes I did, Mom. That was some of the most fun I have had all summer." What the hell was that, he thought to himself? That wasn't the answer he had decided upon? "Besides, I forgot to take a towel with me into the bathroom..." There was the answer he wanted to give her before. Why had that other one popped out?

"And did you have to be show off your erection as you walked around endlessly? Did you have to stroke it before stuffing it into your shorts?" Julie was trying to push him into a corner. What she didn't realize was that she was cornering herself as well. This discussion was going to force the issue, and neither of them would be able to back away from it after it was all out in the open.

"I wasn't that hard." Matt said sternly, again wondering why he wasn't trying to cover up his actions from the morning. "And I wasn't walking around endlessly. I was just looking for something to put on. As soon as I found something, I put it on."

"You could have at least turned away, and been a gentleman about it."

"You could have been a lady, and turned around yourself you know." Matt snapped back. "Heck, you could have left the room.

Why did you stay for so long once you saw that I was naked? And why of all days did you decide to go into my room this morning? I don't think you have been in my room since I started doing my own laundry two years ago. And all of a sudden, on the one day that I forget a towel, there you are gathering laundry from my floor just as I get back from my shower. What were you doing up there?"

"You said it yourself, I was grabbing laundry." She quickly grabbed her plate and the others and headed into the kitchen to wash up.

"So you weren't trying to show me your thong clad ass by bending over, waiting for me to get back to my room and catch you like that?" he accusingly said as he walked up behind her as she fumbled around in the sink. "And what about all of the other times that you have flashed me over the last couple of years?"

"Oh really, my thong clad ass? What do you think I am, honey? Some kind of a slut?" She struggled to keep a level tone. His accusations were spot on, and they were making her even more wet than before between her legs.

"You could be. I haven't seen a wet spot like that between a woman's legs since I took this one girl's virginity last summer."

"Wet spot! How dare..."

"Maybe you should have waited until you were finished messing your shorts before starting that load of laundry?" he suggested as he pressed up against her and slipped his hand down over the crotch of her shorts.

He pressed his fingers into her mound as she rinsed off the last dish from lunch. She let out a gasp and pressed back up against him for a moment, reveling at the moment. She knew it was wrong to let her son touch her like this, and she wanted it more than anything else in the world. She carefully placed the last dish into the dish rack to let it dry as he cupped her breast with his other hand. She quickly placed her hand over his and helped him grope her tit through her t-shirt. She felt his hard cock press up against her ass through his shorts and her own and pushed back against him, wiggling her butt to get it between her cheeks.

"You know what, mom?" he asked as he methodically squeezed her through her clothes.

"What's that, Matt?" she moaned low, in almost a whisper.

"I think that you are a slut for me." He whispered into her ear.

"I think that you might be right..." she was gone now. All of her resistance to this coupling was history, and she was there completely for her son to take.

"Show it to me..." he moaned into her ear. "Show me what a slut for me you are... Drop your shorts, and your panties... Open yourself to me..."

She didn't respond immediately. She was lost in the feelings of his hands on her. It took her a moment to let the words sink into her, but once she got the meaning behind them, she quickly did as she was told and unbuttoned her fly, pushing her shorts and thong over her hips and down to her thighs where she couldn't push them down any farther. She was pressed too tightly into the sink by her son and couldn't reach down low enough to fully remove her bottoms. She could reach back and grab his head, though, and pulled him in for a kiss over her shoulder as he pushed her shirt up over her breasts with one hand as his other frantically undid his shorts and pushed them down.

He backed off of her to push down his shorts and pulled hers down to the floor as well. Looking back up at her legs running up into her ass, he couldn't resist sliding his hands up the backs of her calves and then between her thighs. When he reached her pussy he slid his right-hand fingers across her slit from front to back as his left hand moved over her left butt cheek and started massaging it. He rubbed her lips back and forth along her slit a couple of times before pulling his fingers away and licked her juices off them, enjoying her sweet taste. He then massaged both of her ass cheeks, pulling them apart and watching her sphincter pucker as he did. He used his thumbs to brush across her hole and even probed it a little bit, but not actually penetrating her.

When Matt was finished playing with his mother's ass, he slowly stood up, running his hands up her sides, agonizingly slowly until his thumbs brushed the undersides of her exposed tits. Then he nestled his cock into her ass cleavage, pressing her hips back against the counter again. He turned his palms up to just barely cup her breasts and pulled her back into his chest as he ground his cock into her ass some more. She turned back to him, and they kissed again, sucking each other's tongues, trying to meld into each other.

Julie felt like her son was trying to tease her to death. He had now played with most of her extremities, but he hadn't really penetrated her yet. She felt like she was ready to die of wanting when he returned his right hand down to her pussy and only

played with her outer labia again. Her clit was exposed, and it seemed like he was ignoring it. She broke off their kiss to beg him to penetrate her, but before she could get the words out, he quickly removed his left hand from her tits and bent her over the sink as he rocked back, lengthening the strokes of his cock along her ass until it slipped under her, and was now pulling up against her labia, and moved his fingers to gently rub her protruding clit, finally giving her some of the pleasure that she needed.

"Please honey, stop toying with your mother..." she cried out as loudly as she could, which was almost inaudible. She was out of breath and could barely speak. "You're driving me crazy... Please baby... Put it in me... Please Matt... Please... Please fuck me... Please fuck your mommy..."

"Ok... Mommy..." He emphasized "mommy" as he used his fingers on her clit to push the head of his dick into her cunt. "I'll give you what you want..."

Matt continued to tease her, though, as he only inserted the head of his cock into her. And then he circled his hips around to stir her up a bit, but still not thrusting into her. She whimpered when she realized that he still wasn't fucking her and tried to push back into him, but he just wouldn't let her get any satisfaction just yet by pulling away from her. He grabbed her wrists and pulled them up across the sink to hold her still and keep her from fucking herself against him. He was going to give it to her, but he was going to do it on his terms.

"Tell me what you what, mommy..." he begged her in a somewhat harsh tone, but not menacingly. "Tell your son what you want him to do to you... Tell your baby boy how you want it..."

"Fuck me... Fuck me baby... Fuck me hard..." she cried out, almost in pain from the wanting. "Fuck your mother... She needs it Matt... Fuck her baby... Fuck your mother hard..." He still wasn't sticking it to her as she wanted. He was groping her breasts and toying around with her nipples as his cock sat at her opening, just waiting to be inside her, but he just wouldn't give her what she was begging for. "Oh please god for heavens sakes Matt... Just fuck me already... Oh GOD YES!!!"

Matt finally did as she asked and drove his cock fully into her mid-sentence, but he was still playing around with her. He held his cock still in her as deep as he could get it. He enjoyed the feeling of being sheathed in his mother's pussy, even more than he enjoyed being inside his sister. He was going to keep himself

there for just a bit longer and get the full effect as he shifted around and ground his pelvis into her ass cheeks.

Julie didn't care so much anymore that he was taking his time. Her cunt was full of cock, and she was enjoying him just being there as well. She did wish that he would fuck her already, but now that he had finally penetrated her, she could hold off her needs for just a little bit longer. She was going to fuck her son, and there was no turning back now that he was inside her to the hilt. Julie reveled in the feelings running through her body so much that she hardly noticed he was pulling back until she felt empty again, with just his head at her entrance as it was before. But he didn't pause it there for so long this time. He only held it there for a brief moment to let her know what was coming. He was going to fuck her and fuck her hard.

"Here it comes Mom..." said Matt just before shoving his cock back into her as hard as he could and then pulling it back out slowly again. He continued this for a half-minute or so, pulling out slowly and then shoving back in hard. She had her hands pressed against the backsplash of the sink willingly now to hold herself up, so he let go of her wrists and wrapped his hands around her boobs to pull her back into him as he thrust his cock as deep as he could. He increased the pace of his out-strokes as he straightened up behind his mother, now that he didn't need to restrain her anymore. He used his thumbs to tweak her nipples as he pounded into her harder and faster. He even pulled them out away from her a few times, giving them some real rough treatment. He knew that Jennifer liked it a little rough, and he was going to see how far his mother would let him take it.

Julie and her husband, Steve, had never gotten into the realm of rough sex. They were intense but not rough. He had smacked her ass every now and then, but more playfully than anything else. His nipple pulling wasn't all that hard either. He was mostly a gentle lover at heart, not so much afraid that he would damage his wife, but more the type that wanted to please. So it was a shock to Julie to feel the way that her son was treating her, and even more shocking to her that she was enjoying it. She loved having her nipples pulled so hard, nearly torturing her. She loved having her pussy pounded so hard, with his cock reaching closer to her womb with every stroke. All of a sudden, she wanted to be smacked, but not the love-taps that her husband gave her. No, she wanted to be full-on spanked and spanked hard. But before she could ask her son to fulfill her wish, he started up the conversation again.

"Are you enjoying this mommy?" he asked as he continued fucking her. "Are you enjoying fucking your son?"

She couldn't hold back her emotions or her answer. She just blurted out, "Yessss... Oh fuuuuck yes..." as she pushed back into her son, trying to get him deeper.

"You like it when I fuck you hard... You naughty girl..."

"Yes... I am naughty... so naughty... a naughty little girl..."

"You need to punished... The tables are turning Mom... I'm going to punish you for once..."

He was reading her mind. That was the only way that she could explain it. He was reading her mind, and now he was going to grant her deepest wish to be spanked. He grabbed her hair with his left hand, and she looked back as he pulled his right hand back and brought it down to her ass cheek, hitting it hard. Julie let out a yelp in pain and then moaned in pleasure from it. She hadn't even thought of hair-pulling. But now that it was happening to her, she was into that as well. She repeated her high-pitched yelp and followed it up with a similar moan to the one before as he smacked her ass again, with the same intensity and power as before.

"What's this?" Matt asked before spanking his mother again. THWACK!!! "is my mother enjoying being punished?" THWACK!!! "Does she like her son spanking her?" THWACK!!!

He continued beating on her right cheek as he fucked her and asked her how much she enjoyed it all. She couldn't find the words this time, though. She just continued yelping like a dog when struck and moaning as the sharp pain dissipated, and she anticipated the next strike. She never imagined that she could get so excited from being treated like a slave by her son, her very own son that she was fucking. It just hit her what she was doing, and it hit her hard that she was not only cheating on her husband, but she was fucking her own flesh and blood son. It hit her like a ton of bricks. It was about to send her into her first orgasm of the day. She loved the thought so much.

But just as she was about to go over that edge and let that blissful orgasm wash over her, she heard a car pull up into the driveway. She looked out the window above the sink. Matt saw it too, and quickly pulled his dick out of his mother's cooch. His oldest sister had some of the worst timing sometimes. Matt was glad he hadn't tossed his shorts across the room as he stepped into them and pulled them up while running up to the upstairs bathroom to wash himself off real quick. Julie didn't have any

such luxuries. She had to regain her sense of her surroundings, find her shorts (that were still around her legs), and just as she got them pulled up, she saw Sally opening the door. Julie quickly remembered that her breasts were exposed and pulled her shirt back down over them just as Sally came into view.

"That fucking bitch!" yelled Sally as she stormed into the house, passing her mother and the kitchen as she ran into the laundry room, and continued yelling as she stripped off her jacket and blouse and tossed them into a pile next to the washing machine. "I can't believe that bitch had me fired! I'm going to call my union rep! She's going to have fun with this one! No one likes that bitch, we all want her gone, and I'm going to get her fired while getting my god damn job back!"

Julie was glad that her daughter was so outraged and running around the house like a madwoman. It gave her a chance to clean herself up with a washcloth before asking her eldest daughter, "What the hell are you talking about dear?"

"The one manager at the bank had me fired while we were eating lunch today. She heard about me making out with her nephew at some club the other week, I didn't even know he was her nephew until after the fact, and she had me fired for it. And to top it off, she tossed MY drink onto MY blouse and jacket, which I have to get drycleaned now. That fucking bitch can't do this, and I'm going to get her for it. I'll be the hero of the bank for it too. No one likes that whore, she rides on everyone like she's a fucking god, and it's about time someone got to her the way she gets to all of us."

"Oh dear! I'm sorry to hear that you lost your job, especially over something so silly. I wish you luck getting it back though." Julie said with a smile.

"Are you ok, Mom? You look flushed?" asked Sally, which nearly made Julie run away. But she didn't. She stayed calm and answered her daughter's question as best as she could.

"Yes dear, I'm fine. I was just washing up after lunch when you came barging in. The steam started it, and your screaming must have sent me over the edge. I am now totally exasperated from all of the heat and emotions in the room."

"Sorry Mom. I didn't mean to startle you. I'll be up in my room on the phone with my union rep trying to get my job back. Don't be surprised if you hear more yelling." Said Sally as she went up the stairs and disappeared into her room.

Julie couldn't be more disappointed and yet so pleased at how the day was turning out. Disappointed at how her orgasms kept being interrupted and delayed and pleased at how she had finally seduced and fucked her son. Even though he technically just took her, but she was still pleased that she was finally getting some from him. So what if their first encounter was broken apart by the rude entrance of her daughter? This wouldn't be the end of it. If not today, then tomorrow she should be able to continue things right where they left off, with her son's cock drilling her to the brink of insanity.

## Chapter 03

Steve was very happy with where his life was. He wasn't as young as he used to be, but even at the age of 40, he was still in the same shape he was in when he was 30, which was pretty good for a 30-year-old. His job worked him hard, for long hours, but he liked what he did and was good at it, and the extended vacation time more than made up for the long hours on most days. He lived close to the office, so travel wasn't a problem either. Steve owned a nice car, a big house, and had a wonderful family of two daughters Sally and Jennifer, a son Matt, and his sexy wife, Julie. When he wasn't on the road, he always made sure to get home in time to see them all off to bed, especially his wife, who he loved to slip it to whenever he could.

The only thing that disturbed his perfect suburban life was something that his wife had said a couple of weeks ago. It wasn't anything big, and he wasn't sure if he even believed her, but it had gotten him thinking a lot of things that he normally wouldn't have thought about. She had mentioned suspicions of their son and younger daughter being a bit touchy-feely with each other, and she thought that something dubious was going on between them. Steve didn't see it, though, and he highly doubted that anything was going on with them. They were growing up, and around the age where petty childhood differences didn't seem so big anymore, and siblings started acting like family instead of bickering prisoners of the same warden.

It wasn't the accusation of something going on between the siblings that were getting to Steve, though it did start him paying a little more attention to the goings-on around the house. He noticed how little clothing each of the women living under his roof had been wearing lately and how sexually they had been acting. A few weeks ago, he had two daughters that were his little girls and a couple of angels. Now, after a good deal of retrospection, he could see that for the last few years, they were acting like a couple of sexpot devils. Both Jennifer and Sally were always running around the house in skimpy outfits or wrapped in just a towel. They were always sashaying their hips as if vying for the attentions of men with every step they took.

It was Sally that he noticed more than Jennifer, though. Before her dismissal at work, he saw Sally every morning as the two of them got up at the same time each morning. They showered

right after each other (though in different bathrooms on different floors), and they ate breakfast together each and every morning. Steve would shower first, get dressed, have breakfast, and then head out for work. Sally would shower right after him, show up for breakfast, usually in a panty/tank top set, and head up to get dressed after eating with her father, sharing the paper with each other. If she wasn't wearing underwear to the breakfast table, she was wearing a thin and short silk robe or short shorts pajamas with some tight top of some kind. After work was more of the same, with both of his daughters, they were always running around in their underwear or in some dramatically sexual and revealing outfits. It wasn't like they were overtly showing off, but they weren't trying to hide anything either.

Steve was very perplexed by what was going on. He had kept it out of his mind for a good long while, but he couldn't stop thinking about how there was no way his little girls were virgins anymore, and fantasies about what kind of adventures they must be getting in filled his head on a daily basis now. As the fantasies continued, he stopped picturing so many faceless men getting it on with his daughters, and he started picturing himself with them. He would picture Sally coming onto him as they ate breakfast, or he would imagine Jennifer slipping into the shower with him after a long trip. His mind was all over the place, and he wasn't sure if he could take all of the "innocent" teasings that they had been putting him through lately.

While his father was in agony over what he saw around the house, Matt was in heaven because of it. The flesh he had been seeing from not only his sister's but his mother as well over the last few years had been quite a turn on, and the flesh he had been getting his hands on over the past few weeks was even better. He had caught his sister Jennifer in the bathroom brushing her teeth wearing just a t-shirt, and he lost control, taking her from behind and bending her over the sink, spanking her ass until she came screaming, and waking up their mother, Julie. His mother was another chapter of the same story. She came onto him strongly the other morning until he was forced to bend her over the kitchen sink as she washed their lunch dishes. That encounter had been interrupted by the appearance of his oldest sister Sally coming home early after being fired from her job.

Matt was sure that Julie and Jennifer didn't know about each other, but he had been getting funny looks from Sally the last week or two. They were knowing looks, and they were piercing

his soul. He wasn't sure if she knew about him and their sister or something he had forgotten about, but he was sure that she knew about something, and that was the only recent atrocity in his life that he could recall. Matt was also sure that he could get Sally into bed with him as he had done with Jennifer and Julie. She had been giving him the same looks that the other two had been giving him for about the same amount of time since puberty had made him more manly. If he weren't so sure that Julie and Jennifer were oblivious to each other, he would have thought that all three of them were in on it together, but that was too ridiculous even for this situation.

Matt turned his attention to the sex he had gotten from his mother the day before as he stroked himself before getting out of bed. They didn't finish, though he wished they had, there would be time for that later. He was wondering whether he should go wake up his sister and give her a taste of his morning wood, or should he go to his mother and give her the ending that they both missed the other day. He decided against going to his mother because that could tip Jennifer off that something was amiss. She was probably waiting for him to go to her right now. If not on her way over to him right now.

Then Matt remembered that Sally wasn't working anymore right now and that she was probably in her room down the hall right now. She was seducible, but she could throw a wrench into his affair with his sister if he got caught going in or out of her room. There was a chance he could turn that into something even more fun, but there was also a chance that everything could blow up in his face if not done properly. He was so torn about what was going on in the house. He decided not to go to anyone's room and to just get himself off in the shower before going downstairs for breakfast.

Jennifer was lying in her room, playing lazily and gently with her pussy, wondering if Matt would be making a trip to her room. She, too, was worried about Sally catching them, but not so much as she should have been. She, too, had been seeing those knowing looks from her older sister and was pretty sure that they were about the sex she was having with their younger brother. The amazing, ear piercing, Earth-shattering orgasmic sex they had been having over the last few weeks. She really enjoyed sucking her brother off or letting him fuck her when they could be caught at any moment. She stroked herself more actively as she thought about their encounter in the bathroom the other night. She was completely unaware that she had been caught the second time her brother did her, and that Sally had

seen her get bent over the downstairs sink, and that she had been masturbating to the thought of joining the two of them for the last few weeks.

Sally was awake in her bed too. She heard the shower start and wondered if it was her brother or sister. She didn't hear any doors open, so she was unsure of which room the person had come from. She thought about surprising whoever it was and joining them in the shower regardless of which sibling it was. She never really thought of herself as bisexual, but she was. She hadn't done anything with another woman yet, but she was always fantasizing about getting down and dirty with any number of hot women she had known over the last few years. But what she really wanted was her brother, though she wouldn't turn down a roll in the sack with Jennifer, or her mother, or her father for that matter. Her father.

She had been noticing him looking at her a lot the past couple of weeks. They were leering stares, and they were sexual to the point of giving him an erection when she was around. Every morning for the past two weeks, she had noticed him getting hard at the table as they ate. She wondered how big he was, and if she could seduce him along with her brother, and maybe have the two of them bed her at the same time. When she was in college, two men had taken her at once one night at a frat party. She was bent over the edge of a couch by her then-boyfriend. He went on to urge his best friend to stick his cock in her mouth. They fucked her from both ends for a good five minutes until her boyfriend came in her pussy. And then his friend came around behind her and stuck his cock in her ass. It was her first anal experience, but not her last. She had talked her boyfriend into it a few times before they graduated and split up and had gotten it a couple of times since then. She really enjoyed having a cock up her rectum, and she wanted it from her brother and father now that all of them had crossed her mind so quickly in succession.

As Matt ate his breakfast, he thought about how many times he had bent his family members over the sinks of the house in the last month. He had bent Jennifer over the upstairs sink twice, and the downstairs sink another time. He also bent his mother over the kitchen sink yesterday afternoon. He appeared to have a fetish for that type of thing. If he did get into Sally's pants, he would have to be sure to do it over a sink. Maybe he could lure her into their mother's bathroom, or the laundry room, and get the trifective of women over different sinks?

The moment Matt finished that thought, he saw his mother in a white tank top and a black thong coming down the hall towards the kitchen from one direction, and Sally wearing boy-shorts and a short sleeve pajama top coming from the stairs in the other direction. He had made pancakes for breakfast and assumed that was why they were swarming in on him. He made enough for everyone, not just because he wanted pancakes (which he did), but because he wanted to keep on the good side of his mother, and console Sally over the loss of her job, and make up to Jennifer the lack of any playing around this morning.

"You made pancakes? Oh how sweet of you Matty," said Julie as she hugged her son from behind.

"Yeah, bro. Way cool of you," said Sally as she kissed him on the cheek from the other direction.

Yes, Matt was in heaven as his mother and sister sat down around him and started eating. He had two sets of tits and cleavage to gaze at, as well as his mother's panties and his sister's camel toe. They both seemed to be stealing long looks into his eyes. He wasn't sure who to focus on more, so he chose his food and only took occasional looks at either of the women until Jennifer made her way down to investigate the wonderful scent of food permeating the house. She came down in a white silk negligee and white lace panties. He could see her nipples sticking out, and on the other two as well, but he could also practically see through the lace on her panties. Oh yes, Matt was in heaven as he slowly ate his breakfast.

"So Mom," Jennifer started to ask as she sat down and pulled up a plate of food. "Did you give it to Matt yet for what he did yesterday?"

"Yes Jen, we had a good long discussion after lunch yesterday," replied Julie as she winked at Matt, remembering their experience over the sink.

"I doesn't look like he learned his lesson," quipped Jennifer pointing towards his erection.

"Didn't learn what lesson? What was he getting it for after lunch yesterday? What does this have to do with his crotch?" asked Sally with a perplexed look on her face.

Julie nearly spits the food out of her mouth after hearing the last two questions. All she could think of was how SHE was getting it good and hard after lunch with his crotch. "It was nothing dear, eat your breakfast."

"It wasn't nothing," butted in Jennifer. "Mom was picking up some clothes off of his floor yesterday to even out a load of laundry when he walked in on her after his shower, and he was totally naked!"

Sally had a mixed look of shock and jealousy on her face after hearing that. She wished that she could catch him in the buff like that so that she could take advantage of him. She wouldn't scold him. She would reach out and grab his tool and massage it, and reward him for his boldness.

"Not only that, but he paraded around for like, five minutes with an erection before getting dressed!"

"Five minutes? You saw all this too?" asked Sally, begging for answers.

"No, she wasn't there too," said Julie, trying to diffuse the situation, "and it wasn't five minutes, it was more like one. I already warned him to keep it covered when in mixed company, which he is doing. So don't bother him or me about it anymore." There, she thought. That should keep them at bay for a little while.

"So mom," Sally continued. "How big is he? Did he touch himself at all? Did he touch you?"

"Sally! I think I've heard about enough of that!" scolded Julie, but feeling a little hypocritical, she added with a smile, "He was about seven inches long, and no, he didn't lay a hand on me."

"Did you lay a hand on him?" asked Jennifer, just fishing for some dirt on her mother.

"Jenny! I never!" insisted Julie. "Now eat your breakfast before it gets cold. These really are delicious, Matt. You should make us breakfast more often."

They quit teasing Matt as he finished up his breakfast, but the gossip machine turned on full strength when he left to get dressed for the day. None of the women gave up any private info about what they had really seen or done, but they discussed his package quite thoroughly before splitting up to get ready themselves. Julie had agreed to take Sally out for a celebration of her freedom until she got her job back, and Jennifer was just going to spend the day with friends. When Matt learned of their plans, he made some calls and got together with his friends, and spent the day just hanging with them until late that night. He knew that Jennifer was just teasing him when she pushed things that morning, but he was planning

her punishment all day. He was going to enjoy getting even with her, and he had a feeling she would enjoy her punishment too.

Late the next morning, Sally woke up on top of a bed, naked, with a sore ass. After a quick moment of panic, she was relieved to find that she was on her bed in her room at home and relaxed a bit before trying to figure out what she had done the night before. The last thing that she could remember was being out with her mother and having drinks with dinner. She sat up in her bed and tried to focus on what happened next, but it just wasn't coming to her. She got up and looked at herself in the mirror, and was pleased to see that she didn't have any unusual bruises on her body, and recalled bumping into her friends as she and her mother left the restaurant. "Ok, good, the night is coming back to me," she said quietly to herself, "slowly, but it is coming back, and that's a good sign."

She looked at the clock to see that it was 11:30 am, and the day was well underway already as she tried to recall where her friends had taken her last night. She could picture a club, not sure which specific one (and not really caring, they were all the same around here, and all fun), and she remembered dancing with a lot of men. This wasn't very different from her normal nights out, but she didn't usually wake up with a sore ass. That was why she was trying so hard to remember a night that she wouldn't normally mind forgetting. She tried to remember what had happened after the club, but it just wasn't coming to her.

As she concentrated on what happened when she left the club and with whom, she decided to take a shower and freshen up a bit. She grabbed a towel, and feeling naughty, ran out into the hall and over to the bathroom without covering her naked self up. She was actually a little disappointed that no one had caught her, as she was hoping Matt would see her and make a move on her like he had their other sister, but there was no one there, and her siblings' doors were open, which means they are either in the rest of the house or out for the day with other people.

Sally didn't close the door all the way as she showered. She left it open a few inches so that prying eyes could see, but her shower went by uneventfully. Even after brushing her hair in the buff and waltzing slowly back to her room without her towel, she still didn't see anyone around to witness her naked glory. Deciding that her exhibitionism wasn't going anywhere, she got dressed back in her room and went to the kitchen to have something to eat. She was famished from whatever she had done the night before, and she needed food now.

Dressed in a pair of light blue shorts and a white baby-t, she headed for the kitchen, noticing that Matt's door was now closed. She hadn't heard him come up the stairs, but she was lost in her own world and continued to her destination. Once there, she rummaged through the cupboards before settling on a bowl of cereal and some toast. After sitting down at the kitchen table, she heard someone coming down the stairs and then saw Matt round the corner and proceed to the laundry room next to the kitchen. He went through the load that their mother had probably run through the other day after catching him naked. She wished that she could have caught him naked that morning, or this morning, or any morning.

While watching her brother rummage through the basket next to the dryer, Sally finally remembered a key piece of the night before. Her eyes bugged out as she remembered being bent over the kitchen table and being fucked from behind. It wasn't a clear memory, in fact, it was downright fuzzy, but she was sure that her brother was there somewhere. Seeing him in the laundry was what sparked it, so that was the key. He was in the laundry. "Then who was fucking me from behind?" she asked herself as she ate her breakfast.

"What was that?" Matt asked as he entered the room, changing his shirt as he did.

"I'm just trying to piece together last night," she said after swallowing her last mouthful, glad that she had said that first bit with food stuffed in her face. "I must have been hammered, because I don't remember a bit of it," she said, hoping maybe he would fill in a couple of blanks and especially hoping that he had filled in her blank last night.

"I don't know what you did before you got home last night, but I was out here putting this laundry through the dryer when you got home last night, and yes, you were hammered. I had to help you up to your room after some guy helped you inside." He lied. He was in the laundry room when she got home, and it was morning instead of night, and he wasn't doing laundry. He was hiding in there when the guy she mentioned helped her into the house naked. But he watched from the shadows as the man bent her over the kitchen table. He fucked her from behind before leaving her in the kitchen. Once the coast was clear, Matt showed himself and helped her up to her room, where she immediately passed out cold.

"So you took my clothes off me after dropping me on my bed?" she asked coyly, hoping that the answer was "yes."

"No, I didn't. I don't know how you ended up naked." Which was true. He didn't know. He was actually curious where her clothes were. "Maybe you stripped off in the middle of the night?"

"Yeah, maybe..." she said, a little disappointed that nothing had happened. "so where is everyone? Mom? Jen?"

"Mom decided to start running again. She thinks her ass is getting flabby. Jenny is out with friends at the mall or something." He lied again. His sister was up in her room, just out of view from her open door, and indisposed.

"Ok, well, I guess I'll just have to live with the fact that I can't remember last night," she said as she went back to eating her breakfast. "Unless there is something you left out? Maybe something you're embarrassed about?" She smiled as she finished her sentence, fishing for something that she could use to get him to fuck her. She was sure that someone had fucked her from behind the night before, and if he had been there when she got home, then he had to have seen it or been the one to do it.

"Well, ok, I admit it. You were naked when you got home last night, and weren't wearing anything when I helped you up to your room." Her eyes opened wide with shock when she heard this. Seducing her brother in private was one thing, but showing up at home naked after a night out clubbing was definitely serious, "and I had to grab you by the tits at one point as I carried you up the stairs." He was honest again.

"I think I need to call my friends and find out what happened last night..." she said as she left her plate and bowl on the table and ran upstairs to her room.

On the other hand, Matt grabbed all of his stuff out of the laundry basket and went back upstairs to Jennifer's room, where he found her just as he had left her. She was tied naked to her bed by her hands and feet, with nylons he stole from the laundry and a scarf stuffed in her mouth. Matt smiled as he approached her, remembering sneaking into her room and tying her down. She woke up just as he was securing her left leg, and he quickly stuffed her mouth and told her to be quiet until he was finished.

He was glad that her bed wasn't visible from her doorway in the hallway. You actually had to enter the room to see what was going on in there. He kneeled down on her bed just left of her head and pulled the scarf from her mouth, and told her to be quiet and not to make a sound before kissing her passionately.

His left hand moved down and fingered her as they made out. She pulled gently but firmly against her restraints, trying to pull her brother to her body so that they could fuck, but she was tied tight and could barely move. She bucked her hips up to his fingers as he sunk them into her repeatedly.

"How long do I have to stay like this?" she asked as he broke their kiss, but before he could gag her again.

"Until after Mom gets home from jogging," he said as he kissed her deeply again. "I hope you have an excuse for where you were all morning, for when Sally asks you. I said you were at the mall with friends, so don't contradict me too much." With that, he stuffed her mouth back up again, kissed her forehead, and left the room with the door still open.

Jennifer was really enjoying her punishment. She was tied to her bed, hungry and thirsty. Her door was opened, and she could get caught at any minute. And it thrilled her so much that her pussy was constantly dripping. She laid there spread open for anyone to see if they would just walk into her room. She heard footsteps earlier and assumed they were her older sister's as she padded to the bathroom and back, and then downstairs and back up. It excited her thinking about getting caught, but no one showed up except her brother to tease and caress her every hour or so. No one showed up, that is until she saw Sally poke her head in and look around.

"Jen!" she said, about as surprised as she was when she found out that she showed up naked the night before. "What are you doing tied up?" she asked as she walked into the room and sat next to her sister, taking the gag out of her mouth. "What's going on here?"

"I think that's a pretty long story..." said Jennifer, reluctant to tell her sister the truth.

"I thought that I heard voices before while I was calling my friends. It sounded like you and Matt, but he said that you weren't here, and then I heard kissing sounds, and then someone walking down the hall. I came out to investigate, and found you here like this..." she said in all one breath, trying to piece this together. Her sister tied up all of a sudden, took precedence over her ordeal the other night.

"Well..." Jennifer really didn't want to tell her older sibling anything, but it appeared that she was out of options at this point. It didn't matter, though, as Sally wasn't quite finished yet.

"Oh my god! Did Matt tie you up like this? I knew you two were fucking each other but I had no idea the two of you were into bondage..." It was Jennifer's turn to be shocked. She knew they weren't exactly being careful and suspected Sally knew, but she was never sure they had been caught yet.

"You knew we were fucking?" she asked, about as perplexed as Sally was at the moment.

"Well, yeah.. I kind of caught you two in the downstairs bathroom a couple of weeks ago... I'm sorry, I didn't mean to spy, but it was so hot I just couldn't help myself."

"Wait... A couple of weeks ago? Why didn't you say anything to Mom or Dad?" she asked her older sister, still wondering what she was getting into with this conversation.

"Shouldn't I untie you?" Sally suggested, trying to change the subject, unwilling to reveal her perverted desires for their brother just yet. She reached for the nylon in Jennifer's right hand but was stopped from doing anything.

"No, Matt can't know that you found me." Said Jennifer, almost panicking. "If you didn't tell anyone we were fucking than you have to keep this a secret too. Please?"

"Ok, I'll keep quiet, but you owe me big time for this." Said Sally as she stood to leave. She almost left with the scarf still in her hand, but she noticed it in time and placed it gently back into her younger sister's mouth and closed the door on her way back to her room, and calling her friends.

Jennifer squealed, trying to get her sister's attention, trying to beg her to leave the door open, but Sally never heard her. She was gone in a flash. Jennifer was left alone to come up with an excuse for how the door was now closed when it was left open all morning. "It had to have been the wind," she thought to herself. That was the best excuse that she could come up with. She had to go to the bathroom and hoped that her mother would be back soon so that Matt would let her go.

Julie wasn't out jogging, though. She was in her room naked, spending some quality time in bed with her son. She had gone to bed early the last night fucking her husband half to death. Trying to work off the excitement that she had built up getting started with Matt in the kitchen after lunch, before being rudely interrupted by her oldest daughter after getting fired from her job. Julie needed to climax, and Steve had delivered in spades. After fucking for an hour or so, the two of them passed out for the night. When Steve's alarm woke them the next morning,

they went at it again until he left the door. They started with some sucking in bed, moved to fucking in the shower, and then she sucked him off as he ate breakfast. Since Sally didn't have a job anymore, she wouldn't be getting up early enough to find them fooling around today, and so Julie kneeled under the table and sucked her husband until he got up to go to work.

The next night and morning had followed the same pattern, but with a different order and positions, ending again with her sucking her husband's cock just before he walked out the door for work. She went back to bed, only to be woken again at 9:00 am by her son climbing into bed with her. At first, she thought her husband decided to come back to her for a day off and playing around. But his oral technique on her pussy was different and a little sloppier than normal. But when she looked down between her legs to see Matt happily gobbling up her juices and fingering her cunt she was even more excited than ever. She came for a good minute, muffling her screams with a pillow. After eating her, he crawled up between her legs and fucked her good and raw, giving it to her from several positions.

First, he did her missionary, pounding at her between her legs. She held back her screams of pleasure now, not wanting to give her other children reason to think she was cheating on their father and not wanting to block her view of her son. She wanted to make more noise than she ever had while fucking, but she just couldn't let herself get caught either. She grabbed her breasts with one hand and pulled her son's mouth to her own with her other. She was lost in the moment and groaned into his mouth as she came, but he was still fucking her good and hard, so she flipped them over to ride him.

She bucked like wild, posting up and down on his rigid slab of meat. Now he reached up to grab her tits to stop them from flopping around madly. It was sexy, but it was distracting and threatened to make him cum early. He pulled her down a little so he could chew on her nipples, which made some small yelps escape her lips. She quivered when he bit into her flesh and moaned long and low as she came again. Matt couldn't hold back this time and came with her as her pussy clamped down on him like a vice. He couldn't believe the strength she had down there as she milked every drop out of him with her cunt. They collapsed together and relished the feeling of their incestuous affair.

Matt told her to stay in bed until lunch so that they could play around all morning. He told her that he would cover for her if either of his sisters asked questions, but deep down, he was

sure no one would be bothering them for a while. He knew that Sally had come home just after their father had left for work at 7:00 am and that she would be passed out for at least a few hours. He also knew that Jennifer was tied to her bed since about that same time, as he was grabbing her nylons from the laundry when Sally got home for her morning bang. He just told his mother he was checking up on noise when he would disappear to Jennifer's room to tease her a little, and when he would return, they would play around a little more.

After checking on his sister the first time, he returned to his mother to get a class act blowjob from her. She sucked him into her mouth the moment he neared the bed and pulled on his sack as she swirled her tongue around the head of his cock. She used her other hand to either pull his ass closer to her or to stroke his shaft when it wasn't all down her throat. She was one of the very few women who could take all of Matt's cock. He wasn't huge at seven inches, but it was more than most high school girls could handle. Matt always hoped that he could find some better cocksuckers when he got to college in the fall, but since both his mother and sister could both take what he had to offer, he was pleased with what he was getting on his vacation. After sucking him, she pulled him out of her mouth and placed his cock between her tits. Her husband seemed to always love a good titfuck, and she enjoyed giving them. She was curious about how her son would take it.

Matt loved the feeling and came all over her tits. After finishing and then making out with his mother a little longer, he left again to check on Jennifer and also made sure Sally was still passed out naked above her sheets. He was already planning his story for when she asked what happened. He didn't have the full picture himself, but there was no way he was letting her know that he watched her get fucked by some guy in the kitchen, bent over the table. He had been tempted to take her into the laundry and bend her over the sink in there when her stranger left, but she was too wasted, and he wasn't going to take advantage of someone who couldn't even stand, let alone make a decision of any kind.

This time when he returned to his mother's room, he found her in her private bathroom, washing herself with a wet cloth. He grabbed her, saying there would be time for that later. And then he bent her over her sink to take her from behind. It was his thing. That is what he does. He bends girls over sinks and fucks them until they can't take anymore.

He fucked his mother hard as he looked her in the eyes through the mirror-like he had done to Jennifer the morning before. He grabbed her breasts and pulled her back into him. The flesh of her ass smacked against his abs, and Julie wasn't holding back her moans and groans of pleasure anymore. Matt had told her about Sally being passed out and said that Jennifer was out with friends, so she let loose and gave him everything she had to give. She started screaming loud when he started fingering her pussy and clit, and she nearly collapsed when she came. He had to help her back into the bedroom. He lay her down as he continued to fuck her from above as she laid on her side now. He played with her breasts some more and pulled her leg over his shoulder as he straddled the other one. And he slipped his thumb up into her ass. He toyed with it a little before making her cum again. At which point, he spewed his load into her again. His mother complained about her ass being flabby. He tried to convince her it wasn't, but she was sure that was why there were so many smacking noises between them when they fucked doggie style.

Shortly after that, they heard the shower upstairs running, and Matt went to investigate. He hid upstairs in his room with the door open just a hair to see Sally walking naked down the hall to her room. He then waited for her to go downstairs before following her and having a conversation about her blackout. Afterward, he went up to check on Jennifer and played with her for a bit. Since he had the siblings all wrapped around his finger, he went back to his mother to tell her Sally was up, and 69'd with her for a bit without finishing before telling her to dress for a good jog, since that was the excuse he gave to Sally for her, she was all sweaty and couldn't risk taking a shower until after being spotted.

Matt then left her room and went to watch some TV for a bit. Julie came out of her room first, waiting for Sally to see her in her jogging outfit. Shortly after that, Sally did come downstairs and indeed saw that her mother looked like she had been jogging, as she was all sweaty, out of breath, and very mussed up. Julie said she was going to shower, and Sally said she would make lunch as Matt just sat there pleased with himself. After Julie went back to her room and Sally busied herself in the kitchen, Matt ran up to Jennifer's room to untie her.

When Matt reached the top of the stairs, what he found left him dumbstruck, he was 100% sure he had left her door open when he had left her the last time. It turned him on, knowing that she could be found by anyone who would happen to walk by. In fact,

deep down inside, he was hoping that someone would find her tied up to her bed like that. It would be fun to hear her explain how she got like that and what she had been up to. It also turned him on thinking of her being naked when she was caught. He'd have to ask her what happened to the door and see if she was honest with him.

Matt slowly and quietly opened the door and snuck over to the bed as stealthily as he could. When he reached Jennifer's head, she saw his shadow and looked over at him. It was now 12:30, and her brother was pulling his cock out as he ungagged her. He told her to suck it, and she did greedily. He was still hard from 69ing with his mother, and Jennifer sucked him as hard as she could. She didn't recognize the taste on his cock, though, and made a mental note to ask him about that later. The thought was quickly forgotten, though, as he creamed her mouth and face. He then gagged her again and went down between her legs to her crotch to finger her until she came. He played with her the same way he had played with his mother earlier, as he pulled her lips apart, sucked on her cunny and clit, and even stuck a finger or two up her butt. Jennifer groaned loud at his manipulations of her pussy, and came hard from his ministrations. He then untied her and told her to be careful when pretending to get home. He then said she could explain how the door closed later and left her sitting on her bed dumbfounded.

Jennifer wiped the drying cum off of her face and then looked through her closet for something to wear. She was worried about what Matt had said about the door, but she also really had to go to the bathroom, but it was too risky right now, and she would have to wait until pretending to enter the house without anyone seeing. She put on a simple black miniskirt, a loose-fit white tank top, and a red vest. She opted to go without underwear since she would be going straight up to the bathroom to piss and shower. She could worry about the details after all of that. She carried a pair of heels with her as she peeked out into the hall and then went down the stairs as quietly as she could. She looked down towards the kitchen to see Matt sitting there waiting for food, and guessed that this was her chance to make her entrance. She quickly slipped on her heels and opened the front door.

"I'm home everyone!" Jennifer called from the front door just as Sally rounded the corner into view of the front door, handing Matt a bowl of soup for lunch. Jennifer waved to her sister to

show that she was home, closed the front door, and then ran back upstairs to freshen up.

"That seemed a little rude," said Sally as she sat down next to her brother. "she just ran upstairs without stopping in here."

"Maybe she really had to pee badly, as if she was kept from a toilet for the last few hours?" said Matt with a wry smile, knowing full well that was the reason for it.

Sally let out a chuckle at that as she ate, but then caught herself, trying to figure out how to cover herself. "Where was she then? The mall of 'No Toilets'?"

Matt laughed at that and then left well enough alone. He was pretty sure that Sally had found Jennifer tied to her bed, but he would wait until later to press the issue with either of them. He was fucking Julie and Jennifer, mother and daughter, and would be fucking his other sister soon enough, and he didn't need any of them to find out about each other just yet. He heard the upstairs shower start just before the master bath shower stopped and assumed that his mother would be out soon, while his sister would be another few minutes or more.

"Well, I guess I'll go do some laundry." Sally said as she finished eating. "even if I can't find my clothes from last night, I still have stuff to wash." She still couldn't remember all of the details, but parts were coming back to her. After talking to her friends, she found out that she had been to a party that lasted until dawn. And that a couple of guys had double teamed her right on the middle of the dance floor. She had at least figured out why her ass hurt. She had gotten it in her butt a dozen times or so, but she wasn't that experienced with it, and like this morning, she usually felt sore afterward.

Matt cleared his plates to the kitchen sink and then sat back at the table to wait for his mother and sister to join him for lunch. He had both of them occupied for the better part of the morning and was wondering what they would discuss with each other to cover up their meetings with him. Julie popped out of the master bedroom first, and Matt handed her the meal Sally had left for her. As she ate, Jennifer showed herself and sat down on the other side of Matt as he read a magazine while the two women ate. There wasn't much conversation, so Matt didn't have anything to tease either of them with, but he was still pleased with the way events were unfolding.

While Matt was simply pleased with everything, Julie was ecstatic with excitement. She had received the fucking of her

life over the past couple of days. She was glowing with the fires of passion burning deep inside her. First, she got that teasing fuck from Matt, and then her husband gave her the royal treatment two nights and mornings in a row, and then the marathon fucking she got from her son again this morning. She was as happy as she could be and as well fucked as anyone had ever been. She felt a little guilt from cheating on her husband with her son, but it wasn't anything she was going to let get in the way of her enjoyment. After finishing her lunch, she cleaned the house with a smile on her face the entire time.

That evening Steve came home to his three children and his wife sitting in the living room and chatting with each other around the TV. Yes, it sure seemed like him to be the perfect suburban household. Of course, he was unaware of his oldest daughter having sex in the kitchen just outside his door the night before, or that his other daughter was fucking his son two days ago, or worst of all, that his wife was fucking their son just this morning after he left for work. Steve didn't know about this but was acutely aware that the three women of the house were dressed to kill. His wife Julie was wearing a tight light cream-colored button-up blouse with a loose fit skirt that came to mid-thigh. Sally was just sitting around in her same pajamas as always, the short shorts and short sleeve button-up top that was a little too tight for her massive chest. Jennifer was in the tight black miniskirt and a loose fit tank top that she put on after being untied and looked like a knockout.

Steve was getting hard, looking at all of the female flesh on display around the room. He barely noticed the presence of his son as he walked in and sat between his wife and their younger daughter. He put each of his hands on the thigh of each girl just outside the hem of their skirts and asked how everyone's day was. Everyone lied and said that not much had happened, not wanting their clueless patriarch to find out about their secret perverted love triangles. He was sure that each and every one of them was lying to him, holding something back, but there was no way he was going to get the details out of this group all at once. He would have to segregate them and interrogate them one at a time, and he just didn't have the time, energy, or want to do that tonight. It had been a long day at work, and all that Steve wanted was to have some dinner and fuck his wife into a coma.

Julie reluctantly got up off the couch to prepare her husband's dinner. She was enjoying the way he was rubbing her thigh, but the sooner she made him dinner, the sooner they could get

away from the children for another night of fun. If tonight were anything like the last two nights, she would be in for a real treat when the lights are out later. As she left the room, Steve continued subconsciously rubbing the other thigh he had placed a hand on, not even thinking that it was his daughter's and not his wife's leg.

Jennifer wasn't sure what had brought on her father's attention like this, but she decided to just sit back and enjoy it, hoping that her siblings didn't take notice of his hand on her leg. She was a daddy's girl, and like her sister, had her fair share of crushes on the man; her affair with her brother also had a hand in making her more receptive to living out her fantasies with her father as well. If she could sleep with one, why not the other? Every once in a while, his rubbing would go a little higher than normal. His pinky would slip under the hem of her skirt just a little. It was turning her on, and she found herself wishing that he would just push his hand up and touch her through her panties. Then she remembered that she had neglected to put on any panties after her shower this afternoon and couldn't wait for her father to find that out.

Julie called for dinner in the other room, and everyone stood to go eat as they had been waiting for Steve to get home for their meal. Steve's hand never reached his daughter's sex, but it did pull her skirt up quite a bit as they stood. Lucky for her, they were behind her siblings in the line for the dining room, and she gave her father a smile as she pulled her skirt back down.

"Better be careful Daddy, I'm not in the mood for flashing my nakedness to everyone else right now," she said over her shoulder as she smoothed her skirt down her thighs, and she went to the dining room.

"Did she just say everyone ELSE?" Steve asked himself as he adjusted his dick in his pants. "Does that mean that she wanted to flash me? She's naked under that?"

His thoughts were all jumbled as he sat down at the table and began eating. Julie was a good cook, and tonight's meal was no exception. The food tasted wonderful, but his mind was elsewhere. His attention kept flitting back and forth from Julie to Jennifer. He focused on their cleavage, focused on their faces, and noticed how both of them were watching him half of the time, with naughty looking smirks on their faces. A couple of times, he saw a look or two from Sally, his preferred daughter, but he wasn't getting any firm signals from her

tonight, so he spent most of his time concentrating on the other two.

Dinner was pretty much uncomfortable for everyone in the household. Julie and Steve wanted to go to their room for some good fucking, Matt wanted to corner Jennifer about the closed door, and Sally just wanted to escape to her bed to masturbate and sleep away the memories she had pieced together in the last few hours. After they were all finished eating, they separated off to their rooms, except Matt, who waited behind and followed Jennifer to her room.

"What do you want Matt?" She asked as she opened her door and let him in. "Are you going to tie me up and spank me, and punish me some more for the way I teased you the other morning?"

"You would like that wouldn't you?" he said before pulling her in for a kiss. "No, I was just curious how the door closed itself this morning? I'm pretty sure I left it open when I left you here tied up to your bed, and yet when I returned to untie you, I found it closed shut. But you were still tied down. How did the door get shut?" he asked as he teased his right index finger over her chest and stomach.

Jennifer was breathless, but she managed to answer. "It must have been the wind. You know how it is when someone opens the front door, all of the other doors swing closed sometimes. It must have been from Mom coming back from jogging..." she was really excited and rushed the words out so that she could concentrate on the way his finger was making her feel.

Matt was in turmoil over that answer, though. He knew damn well his mother wasn't out jogging, so that couldn't be the way her door got closed, but he couldn't tell her that he was fucking their mother all morning while she was all tied up in her room. He decided not to press the issue with her and to take a shot with getting it out of Sally later instead as he sat them on her bed. In the meantime, he continued running his finger all over Jennifer's body. His other hand reached around and groped her left tit from behind her. He didn't bring her off, though. He was still punishing her, and he told her so. He got her to the brink of excitement and then left her high and dry.

He went over to Sally's door and knocked quietly before letting himself in. She was glad that he had knocked first because it gave her a chance to pull her hands out of her cunt and pull her shorts back up before he walked into the room. He sat down on the bed to her left; he asked her how she was doing after a long

day with a hangover. She informed him that she wasn't hungover at all today, despite how drunk she got the night before.

"In fact, I might have still been drunk when I woke up this morning. That could be why I couldn't remember anything," she said as she sat there, wishing she had the courage to make a move on her youngest sibling.

"Could be, could be..." he replied. "So what did you think when you walked in on Jennifer tied naked to her bed this morning?" He dropped a bombshell on her, and she let the fact that it was her show.

"She told you? That bitch..." she said as she slumped back onto her bed and covered her sobbing face with her pillow.

"No, Sally, Jenny didn't tell me anything." He said as he rubbed her bare left knee with his right hand, half trying to comfort her and half getting turned on by touching her. "That's actually why I had to come in here. I had left the door open when I left her there, and you had closed it. I knew Mom hadn't been upstairs, and that Jenny hadn't gotten out of her restraints, so it had to have been you."

"You mean that instead of her breaking my trust, and telling you about me, I broke her trust by telling you about me?" she asked with a confused look on her face, pulling the pillow off to the side as her brother continued rubbing her thigh now.

"Pretty much, yeah. Though I didn't give you much of a chance to get away with it." He rubbed higher and higher up her leg, pushing his fingers into the underside of her shorts with each stroke. "Were you surprised to find her naked?"

"A little bit, yeah." She said as she wiped the tears away from her face. "But I was more surprised to see her tied up."

"So what did the two of you talk about?"

"Nothing really... It all happened so fast. At first I asked her why you tied her up, and she didn't say. She just begged me not to tell anyone that I saw her like that." Sally was fully collected now.

"How did you know that I had been the one to tie her up?" he asked, truly puzzled. He thought he had given that bit of info away just now as he confronted her about it all.

"Well... Uh... I guess..." she sputtered, trying not to answer his last question, and then the answer came to her. It was honest

mostly, but most of all, it was true. "I heard the two of you talking from my room, but you said she wasn't here, so when I went to check it out, and saw her like that, I just assumed it was you."

Her answer was good enough for Matt, but he wasn't finished with her yet. "So what did you think when you found her like that? Tied up, naked, and helpless?"

Sally knew now that he was trapping her. That question was asked to see her reaction, and her next answer was very important. It would define their relationship for the rest of their lives. She could lie and say that she was disgusted with them for it, or she could walk right into the trap and admit to him that she was turned on and wanted to have a turn with her stud brother. She was so confused she didn't even notice that his hand had moved up her thigh from her knee and was rubbing her upper thigh along the edge of her shorts, pushing under it a little at a time.

"I don't know how I felt about it." It was a lie, but it was closer to the truth than she should have told him. She should have said that she was disgusted and just remained his older sister for life.

"Sure you do," he said as he replaced his right hand with his left on her leg, and placed his right hand on the small of her back, and pulled her to him, playfully jostling her, but really just trying to touch her and get her a little excited. "It must have been shocking, knowing that your brother tied up your younger sister to her bed naked like that? I know I would be surprised to find you tied up like that, and to hear that Jennifer did it."

"I don't know..." she said as she stood up. She had to get away from his touch, or he would drive her insane. A part of her wanted him to do that to her. But her consciousness was winning the battle right now. "I guess I feel confused about it. A part of me is freaked out by what my brother and sister are doing. And another part of me is wondering..."

She paused just a little bit too long for Matt, so he resumed his questioning. "Wondering what, Sally?" he asked as he stood behind her and tried to wrap his arms around her waist.

"I don't know what," she said, breaking away from him again. She didn't want to keep her distance from him, but she felt that she had to. "I need more time to think about it. I think you should go now."

Matt knew when it was time to quit. Even though his mother had put up some resistance, and his other sister hadn't put up

any, Sally was always a special case, and she would take time to break. He was going to give her all the time she needed, and so he big her goodnight, left her room as she requested, and then went to bed hard and unsatisfied. He thought about going over to see Jenny but just didn't feel like starting anything with Sally awake in the next room, even if she did know what was going on.

After giving his wife a good fuck or two before bed, Steve finally fell asleep at around 11:00 pm. As pleased as he was with life, it was a troubled sleep. During dinner, he hadn't paid much attention to it. But when the women of the house had been looking away from him. They had all been looking at his son. During his dreams, though, this became more than obvious. They weren't looking at Steve at all anymore. They were hanging all over Matt as if he was the alpha male of the house, and Steve was now just the beta male. They were all rubbing themselves against his strapping young body and stripping him of his clothes, and each other. The dream ended in a big orgy between his son, daughters, and wife, and they were all laughing at Steve as they fucking his son.

Steve was glad to wake up before his alarm sounded and turned it off before it had a chance to wake his wife. He showered and dressed as quickly and quietly as he could and left the master suite without Julie ever hearing him. He ate breakfast quickly as well, trying to forget the dream that had disturbed him so deeply. "It couldn't have been real," he thought to himself. "My son isn't stealing my family from me... Is he?"

He was about to rush out to the garage over a half hour earlier than normal when he heard someone stirring in the living room. He looked into the darkroom to see his oldest daughter sleeping on the couch in just her short pajama shorts. She was on her stomach, so he couldn't see her breasts, but they were sticking out on her sides, and her ass was barely covered by her shorts. He could just barely make out an empty bottle of liquor under her hand, hanging from her dangling arm off the front of the couch to the floor. He decided to wake her. He told himself it was so that her mother or siblings wouldn't find her like this, but it was really so that he could see her sit up and see her with her top off.

"Sally, baby, wake up..." he whispered into her ear as he shook her gently. "Sally..."

She stirred a little and rubbed her eyes before opening one of them and looked around. Seeing that she was in the living room,

on the couch, with her father shaking her shoulder, she was curious about what was going on. She felt drunk and was concerned she might be becoming an alcoholic. She was about to sit up and even started the motion until she felt her bare tits pulling across the upholstery of the couch. Indeed, as she looked down in the dim light, she saw that her tits were uncovered and would be exposed if she sat up.

She dropped back down and asked her father, "Daddy? I think I'm drunk."

"The bottle on the floor suggests as much, honey," he said with a smirk and upset that she hadn't sat up yet. "why are you drunk dear?"

Sally thought back to the last night and making out with her brother. She played with herself for two hours, completely turned on, but unable to get herself off, so she came downstairs for a drink to soothe her nerves. She opened a half-finished bottle of vodka, and that was all that she remembered. She didn't know where her shirt was or why she was on the couch still. She should have gone up to her room if she was going to get this drunk again.

"I couldn't sleep," she said in her baby voice. She looked at the clock on the mantel and saw what time it was. "Daddy? Shouldn't you be eating breakfast, and getting ready for work?"

"I already ate breakfast. I was about to leave when I heard you." He said as he placed his hand on her bare back and patted it, "but thanks for caring." After he pats her back twice, he held his hand there, just barely rubbing his palm against her naked flesh. He absentmindedly adjusted his package in his pants as he grew harder, and Sally noticed it.

"Why are you up so early Daddy? Trying to ditch your one night stand with Mommy, and sneak out before the regrets sink in?" she joked. She was laying the baby voice on really thick now.

"Yes, dear. I don't want her other lover catching me here with her." He was joking as he stroked his daughter's back lovingly, but neither of them had any idea how right he was about his wife having another lover. "And besides, I have an early meeting to get to, like all men do when they leave their affairs behind."

"Daddy!... You can't have an affair with your wife..." She was definitely still drunk when she said this, as she was not only taking her baby voice to an extreme, but she was slurring her words quite a bit too. "You would have to fool around with me to have an affair before work today..." She grabbed his package

with her dangling arm after she finished saying that and started rubbing him through his trousers.

"Baby..." His voice was choked. "I don't think you should be doing that right now..."

"How about later than Daddy?" she said with a giggle as she continued stroking him through his clothing. "Don't worry Daddy, I won't tell Mommy about us."

Sally rolled onto her side, finally exposing herself to her father as she reached down to his pants with both of her hands and started undoing his fly. Steve just stared in a mix of lust and confusion as his daughter pulled his cock out into the open and stroked him in the dark living room while the sun came up. She stroked him with both hands as he sat there dumbfounded, but she was still drunk, and took one of her hands to move his hand from her back to her breast, and used his fingers to grope her tit.

"It's more fun when you join in Daddy." She continued stroking him and urged him up onto his knees and then to his feet in front of her as she sat up. "It's always more fun when Daddy joins in." she said as his pants fell to the floor at his feet.

She leaned forward and sucked her father's cock into her waiting mouth. A little bit of drool escaped her lips and hung down to her breasts, while the rest of her saliva was coating his shaft, copiously lubricating him as he slid in and out of her sucking orifice. She stroked what she didn't have in her mouth and massaged his balls with her other hand. His hand had fallen lifeless to his side, though, and she had to stop stroking him for a moment to place it back on her tit and get him fondling her on his own.

Steve was lost in the pleasure of his oldest daughter's mouth. All of a sudden, he was convinced that his son wasn't replacing him as the head of the house. If there was anything going on, and it wasn't all in his imagination, he definitely wasn't being replaced. His daughter wouldn't be sucking him right now if Matt were the alpha male. At most, this was just a restructuring of the family unit. He was impressed with how well his daughter was sucking his unit. He was enjoying it so much he reached down with his other hand and fondled her other breast. He was then enjoying her breasts so much, he decided to free himself of her mouth and stick his dick between her tits and fucked her like that.

"Oh Daddy... You like it kinky..." she said as she held her tits together for her father and rubbed them up and down his length. She gave his head a lick each time it exposed itself to her open mouth. She squeezed her thighs together in time with her breasts rubbing his dick; her shorts were getting soaked through. "Daddy?" she asked, looking up into his eyes.

"Yes... dear?" he asked, out of breath, and loving his daughter's body.

"Could you fuck me before you leave for work?"

"Is she serious?" he asked himself in his mind. He didn't care about the answer to that, though. He pulled her hands from her tits, letting his dick free again. He then pulled her to her feet, turned her around. She was kneeling on the couch and bent her over the back of the couch. Once she was in position, he pulled her shorts down as far as he could, lined his member up with her cunt, and pushed himself in slowly. When he reached full depth with no problem, he realized that he didn't need to hold back with her and began fucking her at a steady but considerable pace. He grabbed her hips and pulled her into him, but if he hadn't, she would have still been fucking him right back with all of her might.

"Oh yeah Daddy... Fuck your baby girl good... Fuck me hard Daddy..." she softly cried as she met his thrusts with enthusiasm. "Yeah Daddy... You fuck me so good..."

He did just that. He fucked her as hard and as fast as he could. He wanted to cry out, as did she, but they held in their moans as they fucked just one room away from his wife, her mother, and Jennifer and Matt a floor above them. He felt ready to explode. The moment was too much for him, and he couldn't last as long as he normally did with his wife. He groaned a little louder than normal, and Sally knew that he was about to cum. She finally had an orgasm herself shortly after they began fucking, so she didn't care if he finished in her or not. She wanted to suck him off now. She quickly jumped up off of his cock, turned around, and sucked him back into her mouth while jerking him off. She sucked until she tasted cream, and then she sucked until there was no more cream left. She showed the prize she had retained in her mouth to her father and then swished it around with her tongue before swallowing.

"Daddy, your jizz tastes so good... and I came so hard on your cock..." she said as she continued stroking his softening member and licking him clean between sentences. "But... it's getting late... and you have to get to work..." She pointed at the clock,

and Steve looked to see that it was indeed time to leave for work. He thanked his daughter for the quickie, told her to put her shorts back on and get to bed in her room. And then he woke up to the sound of his alarm as he realized he was having yet another dream.

# Story 02

# Chapter 01

I was nineteen, and my body was trembling almost unperceptively with anticipation for what was about to happen in this very odd situation.

I watched my mother, Donna, slip the silk robe from her shoulders before laying it on a chair next to the bed. I caught my breath as our eyes held each other for a moment. Then she slowly smiled as she looked at me; she was completely uninhibited as I looked at her nude body. It was the first time I had seen her completely nude, and she looked sensuous in the soft light of the bedroom. Her breasts hung erotically on her chest, and the dark patch of her pubic hair was neatly trimmed and inviting. I was surprised at how comfortable she seemed to be as she stood there, getting herself ready for sex.

She gracefully turned back the covers of the bed and glanced at me again with a relaxed soft smile. Nothing was said; it wasn't necessary. I watched her move femininely around the king-size bed. Her long brunette hair shimmered as it cascaded down over her shoulders and down the pale skin of her naked back. For a woman in her late forties, she was very, very sexy, and I realized that she was deeply aroused about what was to happen.

Suddenly my father came into the room, and it surprised me. He was wearing a pair of white boxer shorts and nothing else. He ignored me as he crossed the bedroom toward his mother. His gaze was held upon her--admiring her lovely, sensuous, naked body as she stood before him. The distinct bulge in the front of the shorts made it obvious he was aroused. He turned toward me and asked one more time if I was okay with everything, and I nodded yes. My mouth was so dry I wasn't sure if I could have answered anyway. He nodded at me and smiled before he took a few steps toward mother and took her in his arms, and I watched as they embraced. Holding each other sensuously, they looked into each other's eyes for a long moment before they began to kiss passionately. I could see their tongues dancing against each other's as their passion began to build. Their kisses and touching became more urgent as they both were getting very aroused, and they began pressing and rubbing their bodies against each other. I watched as mother slipped her thumbs into the elastic of father's shorts and slipped them down, allowing his hard cock to spring up against her

abdomen. I had never really seen his cock before, and now it stood out hard from his naked body. The head of his cock was a deep crimson color, and his scrotum hung down below it. Mother's hand slipped down father's body, and after wrapping her feminine fingers around the shaft, she began to caress and fondle it.

Let me back up a little and tell you why I was sitting in my parent's bedroom, watching them have sex.

It began on a late Saturday night, and my parents were in the den watching television, and I was in my bedroom sitting at my computer looking at some very hardcore porn. I was completely nude, and I was visiting some of my favorite sites, and naturally, I was very hard, and I was edging as I masturbated. I was looking at one of my favorite mature sites. One particular middle-aged brunette woman with her legs spread wide apart caught my attention, and I started fantasizing about fucking her. I was almost past the point of no return and only one good hard stroke of my hand away from cuming. I was surprised when my father came into my room. He just stood in the doorway of my room, and his gaze was at my cock. I was completely embarrassed and slightly confused, and I stopped jacking-off and tried to cover my cock with a sweatshirt that was on the bed next to me. They'd caught me jacking-off before and never said anything about it, so, yeah, they know I masturbate; what healthy young man doesn't? Besides, I've heard them having sex, and I've even heard both of them masturbate at different times in the past. It's natural, but—you know, we just never talked about it before.

Anyway, my father was wearing his robe and was completely cool about it and apologized for not knocking on the door first. He could easily see my embarrassment, and as he came into my room, he tried to make me feel like it was no big deal. "Don't sweat it, I masturbate sometimes too," he said to me. "Your mother and I both do it together sometimes. Almost everyone does and it's a healthy thing to do...you shouldn't be embarrassed. I just apologize for not knocking before coming into your room."

I think I was more surprised at how casual he was talking about masturbation and admitting that he and his mother masturbated together.

He sat on my desk chair, facing me. "I want to talk to you about something," he said as I pulled on my gym shorts and a tee-shirt before sitting on the edge of my bed. "Your mother and I have

tried to be open with you about sex whenever the subject came up, but, well, we've thought that maybe we didn't do enough. With the Internet and sex education classes at school, we know that you undoubtedly know a lot about sex, certainly more than we did when we were your age, but there's one important part of sex that we would like to teach you about." He shifted in his seat as he continued. "You're a young man now, and if you'd be okay with it," he paused, looking at me before he continued. "And it's your decision, of course. "Well, your mother and I think it would be a good idea if you came into our bedroom and watched us while we have sex."

I know he saw the look of surprise on my face as he continued. "In some ways it's the best way to see and understand what sex is all about!"

Okay, I was totally shocked! I didn't know what to say. I sat in the chair, trying to keep my cool and looking as normal as I could like I was thinking about what he'd said. We were both quiet. I didn't know how to answer. So many things were whirling around in my mind, especially having the chance to actually see my mother getting fucked! I looked at him and nodded as I said, "Yeah, okay...that would be okay."

"You wouldn't be embarrassed?" He asked.

"I don't think so...maybe," I heard myself say as I shrugged my shoulders.

"Good, because there's no reason to be embarrassed or nervous about it," he said. "It's a perfectly normal, and a good thing that happens between two people who love and need each other. Your mother and I have talked about it quite a lot and we think it's the best way to teach you about sex, and more specifically, about sexual intercourse. We both agree that it's very important for us to be completely honest about what's happening as we have sex." He shifted a little and paused before he said, "Something else...um, we realize that it's perfectly normal for you to expect you to get aroused and have a hard-on as you watched us. You shouldn't be embarrassed about it. Have you ever seen couples having sex before?" He asked.

"No," I lied. I'd actually seen my cousin and his girlfriend having sex a couple of times (but that I want to save for another story).

My parents clearly thought I was still a virgin. I'd had some sex with some of my girlfriends before — my parents just didn't know it. And I wasn't going to tell them anything different. Now, I'll admit that the first couple of times my ex-girlfriend Jennifer

and I had sex, it was pretty clumsy and not that great. So, I thought that maybe I could learn something by watching them.

In addition, this opportunity touched many of my very, very private fantasies, fantasies that I'd secretly jacked-off to countless times. They centered on seeing my mother nude and seeing her getting fucked or, even stronger, lying on her naked body and fucking her with my hard cock. Oedipus complex? Yeah--maybe. But I don't give a shit what it's called. No one ever suspected that I had fantasies about fucking her, and those fantasies of her made me very horny and set my imagination on fire. My strongest ejaculations were always caused by my lewd thoughts of fucking my mother.

My father stood up and turned toward the door, and when he got to the door, he paused as he looked at me and said, "We're going to bed now and we are going to have sex so if you want to, you can come to our bedroom...whenever you feel like it."

And so, that's how I got there in the bedroom, seated on an overstuffed chair, facing their bed, watching them getting ready to fuck. I'm wearing a faded tank top and a pair of gym shorts, nothing more. My father told me before things got started that it was okay for me to be dressed or naked. It was my choice. I decided to start out dressed or at least in as little as possible. "However you'd be comfortable, it's your choice," I remember him saying. He also said that I shouldn't feel embarrassed watching them, and he reassured me that it was natural and healthy if I got aroused as I watched, and I was free to express myself in any way I wanted. That meant it was okay to jack off if I wanted to.

Anyway, they were in their initial embrace, kissing and pressing their bodies together as their hands roamed over each other's bodies. Mother was gently stroking my dad's cock, and I could see the way she pulled his foreskin up and over his swollen head before pushing it back down again. The way they were standing was blocking my view, but I was sure that Father's hand was gently rubbing my mother's pussy from her pubic hair down to her vulva. As I watched them, my cock was throbbing against the restrictive material of my shorts. But as much as I wanted to, I didn't touch myself, not yet anyway.

They finally broke off their long kiss, and father urged mother down on the bed where she lay on her back with her legs slightly spread apart. Father sat on the edge of the bed, his hands rubbing the insides of her thighs, stopping just below her pussy. His hard cock jerked every few seconds, indicating that he was

deeply aroused about what was happening. After a few moments, he turned to me and said in a soft masculine voice, "Your mother has a beautiful pussy." He ran his fingers through the thick patch of hair that covered her vulva. As I sat there watching them, my cock was making a tent in the front of my shorts, and it was very uncomfortable as it strained against the confines of the material.

Mother began breathing deeply as dad's fingers played with her clitoris and her body began to respond to the fondling that was taking place between her legs. She let out a soft whimper before looking directly at me and saying, "That feels so good; your father knows exactly the right spots to touch...and so should you."

She took another short breath and closed her eyes, letting dad's fingers work on her clit. In a few moments, she opened her eyes and looked directly at me before she said, "Come closer. Sit here on the edge of the bed with us so you can see everything."

Her words sent a shockwave of desire through me, and I stood up from the chair and moved towards the bed. "Take your shorts off—I think you'd feel more natural if you were nude like us."

Without hesitation, I slipped my shorts down and let them fall to my ankles before I stepped out of them. With a quick move, I took off my T-shirt and let it fall to the floor. I stood in the room naked, looking at mother, and she was staring at my cock with a soft smile on her lips. Dad turned to look at me with a smile on his face before carefully looking at my cock and cum-filled scrotum that hung between my legs. "Mother," he said. "Our son's got plenty to be proud of!"

Their behavior was so overtly sexual and unexpected that it clearly threw me off a lot. But then, I realized that I'd never seen or been with them when they were so sexually aroused. I know that my presence, watching them, undoubtedly had a lot to do with it. All three of us were really turned on by what was happening.

I watched as my father slipped his fingers between my mother's labia and spread her cunt lips apart, exposing the pink inner folds of her pussy. He placed the index finger of his other hand at the top of her slit and gently rolled the small ball of flesh that protruded from the lips. "Your mother's clitoris is very sensitive," he said in a deep soft voice. He smiled at me as his index finger continued to push the fleshy nub from side to side. "This is the most sensitive part of a woman's body and pussy,"

he said as mother began to respond to his fingers caressing her clitoris. Father held her lips apart for me to see my mother's cunt. "Here," he said, as his middle finger traced down between her wet lips and stopped where there seemed to be a slight indentation at the bottom of her pussy just a few inches above her anus. "This is the entrance to your mother's vagina, the place where it all happens. It's often been called the entrance to paradise," he added with a wicked smile. He gently pushed his finger into the opening, and mother let out a low moan of pleasure. As he slowly pulled his finger out of her hole, it was covered in her clear pre-sex lubricant. He inserted two fingers into her and began gently finger-fucking her. I was surprised and incredibly turned-on by the wet, sloshing sounds his fingers made as he pushed them in and out of her vagina. Mother's body was clearly responding to the pleasure she was feeling, and she was breathing very heavily, and dad's hard cock was still pulsing every few seconds. The side of mother's foot and ankle somehow had come to rest against my thigh, and I reached down and began to lightly rub them. I suddenly realized that this wasn't just a very unconventional lesson about sex. It was much more, and I wasn't sure just how far it would go.

Dad pulled his fingers from mom's cunt and began caressing her inner thighs as he held them apart. I purposely kept from touching my cock—I was afraid that if I did, I'd cum immediately, and I wasn't ready to cum yet.

"Oral sex is a very important part of sex and both your mother and I love it," my father said as he positioned himself between mother's legs with his face only a few inches from her pussy. "Always concentrate on the clit with your tongue and never be too hard. Some women love to have one or more fingers in their cunts so they are being finger-fucked as they get eaten...it's one of the best orgasms a woman can have when a man knows how to do it right," He said with a smile.

I watched as he lowered his mouth to mother's pussy and began to lick her wet clitoris. Her body responded to the pleasure she was receiving by undulating her hips upward toward dad's mouth in a steady fucking rhythm and moaning softly. After several minutes of father's oral stimulation, her body tensed as she let out a cry of pleasure that seemed to fill the room. "Oh fuck," she whispered. "Oh fuck! That feels so good." She paused as she took in a deep breath. "I'm so close; I'm going to cum soon! Fuck! Fuck! That feels so good. Eat my pussy! Eat my pussy," she cried out excitedly. I'd never heard my mother talk like that, and as much as I tried to hold it back, I started to cum,

and I actually shot several white strings of cum that landed on my father's shoulders and mother's legs, which they ignored.

"Ah, Ahh, Ahhh...Fuck! I'm, I'm cuming! I'm cuming." She sobbed as her body tensed strongly. She let out a loud cry, mumbling something that I couldn't understand.

I was embarrassed that I had cum, and I was especially embarrassed that some of my cum had accidentally landed on them!

Dad pulled away from mom's pussy and slowly stood up next to the bed, looking down at her. His cock was throbbing, and he reached down and stroked it as if he was about to jack off. There were long strings of clear pre-cum emanating out of the opening of his penis that ran to his thighs like soft silver threads. He looked at me and smiled as he reached around to his shoulder and collected my cum with his hand. Then he brought his cum-filled hand down and rubbed it on his hard cock before he began stroking it. I could see several white globs of my cum on his cock as his hand moved back and forth along the length of his shaft, and I couldn't believe how erotic it was. I was surprised that my own cock was still very hard, so soon after cuming. I got off the bed and stood next to dad, looking down at mother, and I began to slowly stroke my cock, which exposed some small traces of my cum that had been trapped under my foreskin when I came.

Mother was still enjoying the lingering effects of her first orgasm, but she managed to sit up on the edge of the bed with her feet on the floor facing dad and me. Our cocks were both pointing at her beautiful face, and there was a slight moment of hesitation before she reached out and took our cocks in her hands and started stroking them. It was at that point that I realized that there was a huge possibility that I would have the opportunity to fuck my mother before the evening was over. Her hand was warm, and she knew the exact pressure it took to use my foreskin to cover and uncover the head of my cock. It's an intense feeling when it's done right, and mother surely knew how to do it right. It hadn't been very long since I'd cum watching dad eat mom's pussy, but I was incredibly turned-on and knew I could cum again.

Mom stopped jacking us off, and she took a moment to admire the cocks of her men before looking at me, saying, "Feed it to me." I wasn't sure what she meant, and she said again, "Feed me your father's cock," Her arms were hanging at her sides, and dad moved a step closer to her so that her mouth was only

inches from the end of his cock. She waited as I took dad's cock in my hand and directed it into her open mouth. Dad moved closer again. We watched as his cock disappeared into my mother's mouth, and he began to fuck her beautiful face.

"Your mother is a hot fucking cocksucker...I've shot a lot of cum down her throat over the years," he said with a smile.

Except in some porn movies, I'd never seen a woman suck on a cock the way mother was sucking on dad. Her head moving rhythmically from side to side and her lips and tongue worked on the underside of his cock. She was moving faster and faster, and dad started to moan with pleasure. I noticed small beads of sweat forming on her forehead, and I couldn't help thinking that she looked as if she was in a sexual trance.

"Oh fuck Donna, suck me...suck my cock and swallow every ounce of my cum! I'm so fucking close...you're such a great fucking cocksucker!"

He and I were standing shoulder to shoulder watching mom, and he said to me, "Look how beautiful your mother looks as she sucks on my cock...it's so fucking erotic!"

She responded to his words by moving her hand up and caressing dad's sagging scrotum, and I was surprised when she reached out and took my hand and bringing me closer. She placed my hand on her left breast. I couldn't believe that I was massaging my mother's breast as she sucked on my father's cock, but it was so erotic I could hardly believe what was happening. Mother was sucking harder and harder as she rubbed dad's balls. She definitely wanted every drop of his cum when he finally ejaculated in her mouth. Dad was moaning loudly, and his hips were softly driving the whole length of his cock into my mother's mouth. He was constantly moaning as his orgasm built in intensity. "Oh fuck! Donna suck my cock! I'm...I'm...Oh fuck Here it cums! Here it comes!"

Suddenly my father began to moan loudly, and he placed his hand on my shoulder, the other on my mother's head, as his body convulsed hard several times, and he began to cum. His cock spewed his white cum down mother's throat as she kept working on him, sucking out every drop of her husband's cum. He gripped my shoulder hard as mother drained his large balls of their precious liquid.

As the intense pleasure subsided, father moved to the bed and lay down on his back as his softening cock flopped over onto his right thigh. Small drops of his cum were still leaking out the end

of his cock, and I looked at mother as she stood up and put her arms around me, holding me tightly against her naked body.

We passionately kissed as she pushed her body against me. We broke off our kiss, and she whispered something in my ear that I never expected. "Do you want to fuck me?"

I just looked at her for a moment, and she repeated the question, "Do you want to fuck me so I can show you how to make love to a woman, I hope you do!" She said. There was a spark of mischievousness as she looked into my eyes. She knew very well that I wanted to fuck her.

"Yes, yes I want to fuck you," I answered.

Mother smiled and said, "Your father and I realized that there was a pretty good chance that once we started—I guess we can call this a lesson--but once we started a lesson we knew there was a very good possibility that it might end up this way—and we're okay with it if you are. I've admitted to your father a long time ago that I was sexually attracted to you and secretly wanted to have sex with you. He understands perfectly and has actually encouraged it. We were just waiting for the right time."

Dad raised himself on his elbows and added with a chuckle, "Son, your mother's a great fuck! She can really teach you a lot. I've always told her that I was fine with it as long as I could watch you fuck her."

I began stroking my cock as I looked at my mother as she lay back on the bed. My mind whirled with excitement. This was so much more erotic than any fantasy I'd ever had, and I couldn't believe it was happening to me. Dad looked at me and said, "Okay Donna, it looks like your boy is more than ready for you."

Mother spread her legs. She pulled her knees up against her chest, causing her vulva to protrude out a little. I moved up between her legs, and I remember thinking that she had the most beautiful pussy I had ever seen—even on the Internet. Dad knelt on the bed next to mom, and he started fingered mom's pussy for a few moments. I felt mom's hand on my cock as she directed it to the very entrance of her vagina. As my cock head rested on the soft folds of her pink pussy, ready to invade her vagina. I couldn't believe how warm and wet her cunt was. "Fuck me baby, fuck me with your handsome cock," she whispered. I immediately pushed my cock into her velvety hole, all the way until my scrotum prevented me from going any deeper inside her. "Fuck me baby," she said to me. "God, you're cock is so big. Fuck me baby!"

Mom had reached out and was stroking Dad's cock as he watched us fuck.

The harder I fucked mother, the harder she fucked me back. Each stroke of my cock into her was met with a powerful response. And the walls of her vagina seemed to massage my cock with strong contractions. She was breathing hard, and she began to loudly moan as we fucked. The urgency was building inside her, and all I wanted to do was keep from cuming too soon and leaving her orgasm hanging.

We fucked hard, but, as I said, my real battle was to keep from cuming prematurely. Mother's rich black hair was matted to her face by her sweat.

"Fuck him Donna! Let him feel what it's like to fuck a real woman!" Father said as he watched us. I fucked her as hard as I could, and she responded by fucking even harder. She fried-out with each deep thrust of my penis into her erotic body.

"Fuck me, baby; fuck your mother as hard as you can! Cum inside me! OH GOD! OH GOD! I'm cumming! My fucking pussy is-- AH, AHHH...NOW, I'm FUCKING CUMMMMING!" She cried out so loudly I was afraid the neighbors would hear us. But the thought was quickly replaced as my cock exploded inside her, and I started ejaculating into my mother's body. "Fuck," I panted. "Fuck! "I'm fucking you, mom!" Dad stared intently at us as my cock was still spurting cum inside his wife's pussy.

Mother's body shuddered beneath me as more of my cum was pumped into her sex-hole. I couldn't believe how intense and almost debilitating my orgasm had been. For me, I learned that jacking-off could never be as intense as cuming inside a woman, especially my own mother. I didn't know what to say as I lay on top of her body, both of us breathing hard—I'm not sure I could have said anything at the time. The feeling was incredible. More powerful than anything I could have imagined.

As I pulled my cock out of her freshly-fucked pussy I saw a trail of white cum oozing out of her hole, it was my cum that was dripping out of her, and I couldn't help but feel good. I wanted to go back into her, but my cock was clearly spent for the night.

Mom, dad, and I lay in their bed and chatted. All of us were tired, and when we talked about what happened, it was clear that this was only the beginning. We all wanted more. It was our shared secret, and no one else would probably understand what we shared.

That was just the beginning of some extraordinary sexual experiences over several years, experiences that included my parents, my future wife, a few close friends, and a few other family members.

# Chapter 02

The next morning at breakfast, things were surprisingly normal. Everyone was cheerful, but what happened the night before was obviously on everyone's mind. I knew it wasn't because anyone was embarrassed or feeling guilty; it was really quite the opposite. The feeling was that the three of us were completely relaxed and okay with it. What took place in my parent's bedroom that night had a definite impact on our family. All three of us were affected by it, each in our own way. I came to the conclusion that mother now had another man that she could have frequent and very uninhibited sex. Father was free to enjoy his wife on a new and deeply erotic level that included acting out some of his long-held and deepest fantasies. The strongest included watching his wife as she was being enjoyed by another man. For me, I was wildly fortunate to be having frequent sex with an erotic, beautiful, sensitive, mature woman any time and almost any place we wanted. The fact that she was my mother. I admit that that was even more of a turn-on.

What had happened in their bedroom the night before was well-planned and certainly not a shock to my parents; after all, they were the ones who set it all up under the guise of teaching me about sex. What I didn't know was that for years they'd talked, and even fantasized, about expanding their sex lives to make it more enjoyable by stretching the limits. This included exploring sex with other couples and even singles, but for various reasons, they just hadn't acted on it before.

We'd finished breakfast, and dad and I were still sitting at the small kitchen table as mother cleared the last few dishes. The three of us chatted as if nothing had changed, just a normal morning. Once, as mother bent forward slightly, her robe opened enough that I caught a quick glimpse of her naked right breast and nipple. My stomach tightened with lustful excitement, but I tried not to let it show. When everything was done, my mother left the kitchen, and dad and I continued to sit at the table, making small talk about nothing important. Dad was wearing his usual weekend attire consisting of a bathing suit and a t-shirt. Our conversation so far had politely skirted around what happened in their bedroom the night before. After a lull in the conversation, dad looked directly at me and, with a slight smile, said, "How did you enjoy your lesson last night?"

It was a simple and direct question, typical of him, and I was relieved that the subject had finally been raised even though I didn't quite know how to answer it, "Um, fine," I said awkwardly.

"Just fine?"

"Um, no it was incredible...everything was incredible...really," I said.

"Well, I have to tell you that your mother and I thought so too. It was good sex for us and we'd like to do more if you're okay with it," he paused for a moment looking directly at me. "Your mother and I have always had a good sex life but often there were times that she needed more than I was able to give her, but she never complained. In the past few years she seems to need more and more sex." He paused. "A few things have happened that made us make the decision to do what we did last night. We were pretty sure you'd be okay with it."

I wondered what he meant about a few things that happened but didn't ask. I knew I'd probably find out later anyway. "I'm very okay with what happened...I loved it!" I said enthusiastically. "When you first told me in my room, I guess I didn't really know what to think, I mean I thought I'd be embarrassed watching you and mom having sex but I wasn't. I couldn't believe how good everything felt...mother was incredible—I wasn't embarrassed at all."

He nodded. "Your mother is a very sexy woman, and she loves and needs a lot of sex." He looked down at his hands for a moment before looking back at me and saying, "We've talked about having another man or a woman or even a couple, join us but your mother's still a little reluctant about it. We both realized that you're mature for your age, and the more we talked about it, the more we thought it would be a perfect solution to have you join us for sex. It's fun and a good way for you to learn about sex from your mother and me. Your mother feels safer keeping it in the family." He smiled at me and winked as he added, "This arrangement will let your mother be more open to trying new things and getting a little more adventuresome...kinky," he said with a smile. "She's always wanted to experiment a little. Then he added, "She's on birth control, so there is no worry about her getting pregnant. Another nice benefit of her being on the pill is that, since your mother doesn't like condoms, all of our play is bareback."

Dad took the last sip of his coffee. I was surprised at his complete openness about what happened. "I'll be very honest

here," he said. "I was surprised that it was such a strong turn-on for me to watch and listen to the two of you having sex. It's been a long time since I've seen your mother as turned-on as she was last night and her orgasms were stronger than she's had for a long time."

"I loved it a lot, her body's incredible and it felt really good to fu -."I hesitated to say the word.

He smiled at me and finished my sentence, "Fuck her? It's okay," he said. "You can say it, that's what you and I both did...we fucked her! We fucked your mother. And believe me, she's a woman that can keep us both satisfied and cuming."

He stood up from the table, taking his coffee cup, and placing it in the sink. As he did, I couldn't help but notice the large and awkward looking bulge in his bathing suit that he didn't try to cover. Obviously, our talk had the same effect on him as it did on me.

"I'll be in the spa," he said before going out the kitchen door and onto the patio. We had no close neighbors near the back of the house, and the garden behind the house afforded total privacy. I sat for a moment, thinking about what was happening and what dad and I talked about. I had the feeling they were holding something back, and all I could do was to wait and see what happens.

I finally got up from the table and went to my bedroom. As I passed by the bathroom, I heard my mother taking a shower. I couldn't help imagining what she must look like as the hot water poured down over her naked body.

I'd made plans earlier in the week to go to the beach with my cousins Jason and Brianna; they're brother and sister and, even though I didn't feel like it, I couldn't get out of it. Besides, I actually thought it might be a good diversion from everything that had happened. I always loved going to the beach with them. The three of us went almost every weekend during the summer. Sometimes, I thought the only reason I went was that I got to see Brianna in a bikini. Jason and I are the same age; Brianna is a year older than us. The three of us spent a lot of time together while we were growing up, and the three of us have always been close, a lot closer than most cousins I knew. Brianna is pretty, with long brunette hair and dark eyes. Her tender looking breasts were small and full, and I could only imagine what they must look like under her bikini top. For as long as I could remember, I'd hidden the fact that I had a serious, and I guess, harmless crush on her. The older she got,

the more attractive she became. I've spent countless hours fantasizing about her as I masturbated. I'm positive that Jason knew how I felt about his sister, but he was cool about it and never said anything. Jason and Brianna spent so much time together that neither one of them seriously dated anyone else, but that was their business.

When we got to the beach, it wasn't very crowded, and after setting up, we went through the rituals of applying sunscreen to ourselves. As the day went on, it was very relaxing, and the sun and water felt good, but I constantly kept thinking about what had happened the night before. What was it, I wondered, that made my parents decide to take me into their bed under the pretext of teaching me about sex? I didn't have the answer.

At times it seemed like it was all a very real dream, and whenever I thought about it, my cock would start to get hard, forcing me to turn over and lay face down on my towel on the sand.

At one point, Brianna went down to the water, leaving Jason and me on our towels. Jason looked at me with a grin and quietly said, "Did you see that blond woman in the green bikini that walked by here a few minutes ago?"

"No, I must have missed her," I said.

"You missed it alright," he said with a chuckle. "Nice tits, very nice ass and a bikini that barely covered her pussy...she's got to be in her forties but boy I'd fuck her if I had the chance."

"No, I must have missed her," I said again.

"Too bad...she was a nice looking woman for her age, but fucking a woman like that would be like fucking your mother if you know what I mean...but then, maybe a guy fucking his mother isn't such a bad thing especially if his mother looked like that!"

His comment sent a shockwave through me, but I didn't let it show as my mind raced. Why did he say that? Does he know something? Did I slip and say anything? After all, his mother and my mother are sisters, and they're extremely close, and they share everything.

I got mad at myself for being a little paranoid, and I realized that he probably didn't mean anything by his remarks. I just passed it off as Jason's typical weird view of the world.

When I got home from the beach, it was after 7 p.m., and my parents were gone. There was a note on the kitchen table telling me that they were having supper with some friends and a shock of disappointment ran through me. I went to my room, took my clothes off, and got into the shower. As the hot water poured down on me, I gently stroked my cock for no other reason than it felt good. I didn't want to cum or even get close to cuming; I wanted to save it for my mother's pussy. After toweling off, I went to my room and got on my computer to play a few games, but I lost interest pretty quickly. I surfed the Internet looking for sites about mature sex and found a lot of them featuring mature women and younger men together. The photos and stories really turned me on. My cock was hard, and a large amount of pre-cum was already oozing from my foreskin.

I was suddenly curious about what my parents might have hidden in their room, and since they weren't home, I thought I'd do a little snooping. Their dresser drawers were full of underwear, tops, and T-shirts, pretty normal stuff. After going through each one of the drawers, I was very careful to leave everything exactly as I found them. In my father's bedside table, there was a bottle of KY lube in the drawer, and that didn't surprise me much. I figured I'd petty much drawn a blank, and just as I was about to close the drawer and leave the room, I saw a flash drive at the very back of the drawer. I took it back to my room, put it on my laptop, and opened it. There were what seemed like hundreds of files full of photos of homemade porn. There were also many video files, and I noticed that one of the video files had yesterday's date on it. I started to open the file when I heard my parents' car pull into the driveway. I grabbed the flash drive out of my laptop and ran down the hallway to return it to the drawer. And then back into my room before they got in the house. I couldn't help but wonder what was on the flash drive; someday, I would have to find out.

After getting home and putting on more comfortable clothes, my parents went into the den to watch television, and I went into my room to surf the Internet. About 10 o'clock, they turned off the television, and I heard them coming down the hallway toward their bedroom. They stopped at my door and knocked softly. When I opened the door, they were both standing there looking at me, both nude, and my father had a hard-on. "Your mother and I already started some foreplay in the den," there wasn't much on television, he said with a soft laugh.

Mother took father's cock in her fingers and said with a soft laugh, "Were going to bed to take care of this little problem your father has...would you care to join us for another lesson?"

My stomach jolted with excitement, and I did a pretty good job of hiding it. "Yeah," was all I could say, and I took off my T-shirt and gym shorts and threw them on my bed. I pulled my t-shirt over my head. I noticed that both of them were looking directly at my cock. Mother took my hand and led both my father and me down the hall to their bedroom—the whole time, my eyes were focused on mother's sweet looking ass, and I couldn't help but think about Briana.

Entering their bedroom, mother got on the bed and sat with her back leaning against the pillows propped up against the headboard. She spread her legs, completely exposing her pussy to my father and me. She closed her eyes and tilted her head back as she took a deep breath and let it out slowly. "I love this," she said softly.

"Let me show you your mother's favorite way to be played with during foreplay," my father said as he sat on the edge of the bed facing her. I stood next to him, and my cock was already dripping pre-cum as my father put his fingers on mother's pussy lips and, parting them, held them apart, and I could see mother's swollen clitoris nestled in the pink flesh of her cunt. Father began flicking very lightly at her swollen nub with his fingers before he began stimulating it by rubbing it in a gentle circle. He was using a very light touch as mother let out a soft moan of pleasure. After a few moments, he let his fingers travel down from her clitoris toward the entrance of her vagina, where he stopped momentarily. With his middle finger, he gently inserted it into her, and she responded with a loud moan of pleasure. He brought his finger up he went back to rubbing her bright pink clit.

Her pussy was so beautiful, and I wanted to fuck her so badly, I could hardly wait.

Father slowly brought his finger down and was gently finger-fucking my mother's vagina. The wet sucking sounds of his fingers, working in and out of her vagina, made my stomach tighten with lust, and my breathing become erratic. "Like most women, the hornier your mother gets the wetter she gets, and, your mother is very horny right now...she's ready for you to fuck her," he said. He stood up from the bed and moved a little to the side. As I started to get on the bed, his hard cock slowly brushed against me, and I was surprised at how hot it felt. He

was dripping pre-cum, which stuck to my hip as I got on the bed next to my mother.

Mother's face and warm smile were full of life as she spread her thighs wider apart—inviting me to come and fuck her—fuck her physically, mentally, emotionally, and even spiritually. "Come fuck me baby," she whispered.

I positioned myself between her legs. At that moment, my cock was dangling and throbbing several inches from the entrance to her vagina. Her breast was delicate and erotic looking, and I leaned down and took the nipple of her left breast in my lips and gently sucked on it—secretly wishing a few drops of milk would somehow appear.

I was surprised as I felt my father taking my cock in his hand and gently directing it toward my mother's wet pussy. I didn't care who was holding my cock at that moment—it just didn't matter. All that mattered was that I was only moments away from sexually possessing my mother as my father stood by watching and fondling himself—waiting for his turn to fuck my mother.

It is so hard to describe the feeling as my cock slowly entered my mother's vagina. The velvety walls are warm and yielding, and it's a feeling like nothing else in life. Mother's breath mingled with mine as we began to fuck. "It feels so good to have you inside me baby, fuck me," she whispered again.

Father sat back on the edge of the bed and watched us. Reaching out, he began lightly rubbing mother's breasts, paying close attention to her erect nipples. With his other hand, he was gently stroking his hard penis as he watched my penis going in and out of his wife's (and my mother's) cunt. I put my arms on both sides of her shoulders and lifted my upper body up as we continued to fuck. As I looked down on her, I saw that her face was soft and beautiful and full of lust. She was panting and moaning, sometimes crying out as my cock pounded her responding pussy. "Fuck me baby, yes, like that, yes...oh god your cock is so hard and hot...fuck me baby...I'm so close...oh, fuck me harder...harder...baby!"

To my disappointment, I was getting closer and closer to my first orgasm, and I was trying everything to keep from cuming too soon. Suddenly, I was surprised to feel my father's hand caressing my scrotum, and I couldn't hold back any longer. I began slamming my cock into my mother's pussy as hard as I could, and she met every one of the hard strokes with passion. My orgasm slammed into my body with an incredible amount of power just as my mother cried out loudly and began clutching

at my back. "Oh fuck baby! Fuck Me! I'm cuming baby! Fuck me harder!"

My cock felt as if it was about to explode a few seconds before it began to spew the white, milky streams of my sperm inside the complete darkness of her vaginal canal. Mother's body was jolting and shaking as her orgasm tore through her naked body—my sperm filling her. She moaned and cried out loudly as the intense moment took control of her.

I lay on top of her as our bodies slowly recovered. I smelled her warm, feminine breath as we lay face to face. We looked into each other's eyes, and at that moment, we both knew that we shared something intensely intimate that no one else would ever understand. We had sex, but it was more; we shared our vulnerability and trust with each other. We each carried something of the other within us that would never be lost.

I moved away from her as my father moved in and knelt between her legs. I watched as a large, white glob of my cum slowly appeared at the opening of her vagina, and father gently scooped it up with his fingers and spread it on his hard cock before leaning forward and pushing it into mother's freshly fucked pussy. My cock never really got soft as I watched them fuck. There was something so special about watching my parents fuck, especially when they're using my cum as a lubricant.

We spent the next few hours having sex and playing. It was obvious that this new adventure made my parents happy and relaxed. I loved it and couldn't get enough of our family play. We all learned a lot about each other and what we find erotic.

Little did I know at the time what delights my Sex Education and the mystery Flash Drive would eventually bring me.

## Chapter 03

At first, I thought that my parent's idea of teaching me about sex was just an excuse to let them feel that it was okay to have me join them in their bed for sex, but very quickly, I came to realize that wasn't really what it was all about. The three of us were completely open and honest about sex, and we often shared our feelings, fantasies, family secrets, and deepest desires during those hours that we spent in bed. So often, after having sex, we would lie in bed and talk about it. My parents put a very human face on sex and sexuality for me, and it finally dawned on me that in their own way, they really were giving me an honest, realistic sex education.

My mother is extremely sexual. She loves sex and will do almost anything that feels good to herself and her partner (sometimes partners, I later found out). But, her sex life is well hidden outside of the bedroom. So much so that none of her friends would even recognize the sexual side of her and what she does in bed. She's feminine, ladylike, smart, outgoing, and she's done a lot to teach me about making love to a woman.

My father is a good match for my mother. I learned pretty quickly that he's, well, more unconventional, okay, kinky about sex and what turns him on. He enjoys some bi-play, toys, erotica, and watching his wife being pleased. He's a voyeur and comfortable with it. He's masculine and honest about what gives him pleasure. Their shared fantasies, as a couple, are important to them.

I've come to understand that my parent's relationship, while not like most couples, is so strong and full of understanding that their very unconventional sexuality and shared pleasure doesn't threaten their marriage in any way.

Nudity is something my parents really love, so naturally, we almost always have sex in the nude. Sometimes, when she's feeling especially horny, my mother will wear spiked high heels, stockings, a white lacy, feminine garter belt, and a bra with cut-outs that allow her sensitive nipples to be exposed. Other times she's been known to wear nothing but her crotch-less panties; whatever mood strikes her is wonderful to me.

It was a hot Friday afternoon, and I'd gotten off from work early, and I was home doing some chores. I planned to go to the beach

with Jason and Brianna on Saturday, so I had to get things done before I could go. My last chore was to clean the spa, and when I was finished, I went into the house to shower and cool down. After my shower, I toweled off and wrapped the damp towel around my waist before I came out of the bathroom. I heard my parents in the den and, as I entered the room, I saw that they were sitting close together on the sofa. A porn DVD was showing on the TV screen, so obviously I decided to join them. My father's shorts were on the floor, and his cock was standing straight up as mother slowly stroked it. Mother was wearing nothing but an oversize white tank top and sandals. The way she sat on the sofa, her pink pussy was clearly visible to me, and I was sure that, for as long as I lived, I would never get tired of seeing her pussy. This, by the way, immediately caused my cock to throb to its full stiffness. I'd dropped my towel on the floor and was massaging my cock as I watched them, and I couldn't help but think about the way Brianna looked in her bikini the last time we were at the beach. It seemed strange that I was on the sofa stroking my hard cock, and only a few feet away, my mother was jacking my father off. Her naked beautiful pussy was in full view to me, and I was thinking of my cousin Brianna in her bikini?

After about five or ten minutes, mother reached under one of the pillows and found the vibrator she'd placed there a little earlier. It was about eight inches long with very realistic looking pink flesh. She turned it on, and she began gently running it along the underside of father's hard cock and his scrotum. His attention was riveted to the sensation and sight of the realistic looking vibrator in mother's hands, giving him pleasure.

Father was starting to moan softly as his hips began to thrust forward and back slightly, he was getting closer to an orgasm, and she knew it. She positioned the vibrator against the underside of father's cock as she wrapped her fingers around them both. She was using the vibrator to jack him off. With firm strokes, I watched as mother made the vibrator slide up and down with her fingers as she held it against the smooth, somewhat loose skin of his cock shaft. Father was moaning loudly as his body strained against the pleasurable feelings that mother was giving him. Several minutes later, it was obvious that he was only moments away from ejaculating. His moans were loud, and I noticed that his shaft was a bright red, and the head of his cock was a deep crimson color. "Ohhh fuck! I'm cuming...I'm cuming!" He said loudly with a groan. The first long spurt of his white cum shot from the opening of his penis and landed on his belly and mother's hands. The second and third

spurts landed on his thigh and his belly, and I was fascinated as I watched the thick, white, liquid cum slowly run down and fill his bellybutton. His fourth ejaculation ran down the side of his cock and onto my mother's fingers. Mother took the vibrator away and continued to gently stroke his shaft as the last drops of father's cum drained from his cock. Mother leaned down and took his cock in her mouth and cleaned up the gobs of cum that were still clinging to his cock. My cock was so sensitive that I could barely touch it for fear that it would cum, and I wasn't ready to cum quite yet, at least not by jacking off.

About an hour later, my parents left to do some shopping, and I knew that they would probably be gone for a couple of hours. I was finally going to be alone, and I immediately thought about the flash drive in the bedside cabinet on my father's side of the bed. I realized that this would be a perfect opportunity to finally see what was on it. I knew it was porn, but I had a pretty good idea that there was more than just regular porn. As I started toward their bedroom, my cell phone rang, and I swore softly. I saw that it was my cousin Jason. As I answered the call, I suddenly remembered that we were supposed to go to a movie that afternoon.

"Hey, where the hell are you. Are you on your way?" Jason said after I answered.

"Jesus Jason, I don't think I can make it today," I said.

"What do you mean?" He paused. "You have to make it. Brianna's friend Cindy, you know, Cindy with the big tits is coming with us...shit, I've been trying to get a date with her for months and she finally agreed so you can't screw this up! I need you to keep Brianna company and maybe even a little distracted. If everything works out, Cindy Big Tits might even go to the beach with us tomorrow."

"Hey Jason, I can't—"

"Don't screw this up for me you gotta come...besides, if you come I'll show you some naked pictures of Brianna in the shower," he said with a laugh.

I wasn't sure if he was serious, but I just laughed it off, trying to sound natural.

I got dressed in a hurry, and I couldn't help thinking about the flash drive and, of course, Brianna. Why would Jason say what he did about Brianna to me? Did he know how I really felt about her? Maybe I didn't hide it too well. Did he know how much I

wanted to fuck her, or how many times I'd fantasized about his own sister as I jacked off?

I met Jason, Brianna, and Cindy at the movie and because I was late, the movie had already started, so we decided to have something to eat and catch the next showing. We had a good supper, and we were having so much fun that we almost missed the next showing. Cindy was really nice and really did have a magnificent pair of tits. So much so that Jason practically had his tongue hanging out during the whole dinner. In the theater, as pre-directed by Jason, I sat between Cindy and Brianna. "So the girls wouldn't spend too much time talking to each other," he said quietly to me. We both knew he had other reasons, but I let it go at that.

After the movie, we went to The Writer, our favorite coffee hangout, and spent a couple of hours until Cindy had to get home, so Jason took her, and I took Brianna home. As we drove to her house, we chatted about the usual stuff, and yet, in the back of my mind, I couldn't help but wonder what she and Jason would think if they only knew what was happening at my parent's house at night and what they would think about my sex education.

I dropped Brianna off at her house, and as I was driving home and I was thinking about everything that had happened between my parents and me. What surprised me was the suddenness of it all. More specifically, how things had changed. My relationship with my parents was completely different, and it happened almost overnight. My parents showed a side of themselves that I'd never seen before. They were completely open and uninhibited about sex, and they were anxious to share it with me. If you had asked me a few months ago if I thought I would ever watch my mother jacking my father off on the sofa with her sweet pussy in full view as I watched, or that I would fuck my mother as my father watched? I would have thought it was completely impossible—hard to even imagine. Yet, it's all happening, and it's a huge turn-on for me. Every time I think about the sex with them, my parents, my cock gets hard.

When I got home, I saw that my parents were already in bed. As I walked down the hallway toward my room, I saw that my parent's lights were on, and as I passed by their room, and I saw them in bed. They were lying on top of the covers, both nude and fondling each other. They didn't seem to be in a hurry to have sex; they both just seemed to be enjoying the foreplay.

They stopped as I came into the room, and my mother asked me how the movie was, and we made some small talk. She asked me how Jason and Brianna were and some questions about Cindy. Mother's legs were slightly parted, and I could barely see pussy as she lay there. My father got up and went into the bathroom, and my mother asked if I wanted to join them, and I readily agreed. I was very horny and naturally wanted to fuck her or at least watch her get fucked. I went to my bedroom and got undressed, and went back to their room. As usual, my cock was hard, but so was my father's. At first, the three of us just relaxed and talked, mostly about sex, but not totally. I seemed to have had a constant hard-on, but I was okay; I wasn't embarrassed.

Mother was rubbing both of our hard cocks as she lay between father and me. Father surprised me a little when he asked me if I knew what DP is.

I was surprised by his frankness, and I admitted that I'd seen some photos and videos on the net.

"It's one of your mother's favorite things, she doesn't get enough of it," was all he said.

Mother began fondling dad and me with more urgency; it was easy to see that she was very aroused. Finally, she moved down between my legs and took my cock into the mouth, and started to suck on it. At first, she concentrated on the head by using her tongue on the rim and the sensitive underside. Slowly she took it deeper and deeper into her throat. She sensed that I was getting close, and she varied her technique, which really held my first orgasm back. She is that good! I remembered how I looked down at one point, and I saw her saliva dripping from her mouth and running down the shaft of my cock.

Mother finally moved up and straddled my hips as she positioned her vaginal above my cock. My father took my cock in his hands, and after rubbing the head gently over her pussy lips, he held it at the entrance of her vagina. Mother slowly lowered her cunt down on my cock until it was completely inside her. She looked down at me with a warm smile as she hesitated for a moment. Moments later, she began raising and lowering her body as she fucked my cock. She was fucking me gently as if to take the time to enjoy each special stroke into her body. I remember looking up at her and thinking how erotic she looked with my cock buried deep inside her. I was truly lost in the moment, enjoying the special emotion between my mother and me as we bonded and fucked each other.

She gently leaned her upper body down on mine, which caused my cock to fill her vagina at a different angle. Our faces moved closer until our lips met, and our tongues probed each other. Her breath was sweet and warm. And I realized that my father had moved in behind her and was rubbing KY lubricant on her anus. He put a large glob of KY directly on her anus and worked it into her rectum, and I felt it when he slipped two fingers, coated with KY, into her hole. She and I continued to kiss and passionately fuck as father got his wife's anus well lubricated and ready to be fucked.

My father got into position behind my mother's ass and started pressing the swollen head of his cock against the tight ring of her anus. Mother started whimpering as father slowly pushed his cock into her tight hole. The deeper he went, the louder she became. "Oh my god! Push it in deeper! Push it all the way in my ass! Fuck me! Fuck me! It's such an incredible feeling to have both of my men fucking me at the same time!"

This was the first time I'd ever done it, and I was really surprised that I could feel the head of my father's cock rubbing against mine. It felt as if there was only a thin membrane separating our cocks as we fucked mother. Each time father's cock thrust inside her ass, the head of his cock would bump against mine. It was way too intense for me to handle for very long, and I knew I was about to cum. My father was banging into my mother's ass with a steady, powerful rhythm, and she was moaning loudly, and I completely lost control. My orgasm hit me so hard it surprised me. I cried out loudly as my cock began spurting my hot cum into my mother's vagina. Her body reciprocated by triggering an orgasm inside her as her father kept pumping his cock into her sweet anus. The harder he slammed into her, the more she liked it and, as she admitted later, the stronger she would cum.

My cock was softening and starting to slip from my mother's vaginal grip as they continued to fuck above me. Mother's tits were pressed tightly against my chest, and small beads of sweat were appearing on her forehead. "Fuck," she whispered roughly. "Your father is fucking me in the ass...it feels so good! I'm so fucking close; I'm going to cum again."

I put my arms around her and held her as father fucked her even harder.

"I...I...I...OH...FUCK, I'm cuming! FUCK ME HARD! PUSH IT ALL THE WAY IN!" She shouted as her body was slammed by another of her powerful orgasms. After the initial wave of exquisite pleasure ripped through her, her body would shudder each time

another powerful wave of pleasure would run through her. The sexual power that was in that room at that moment would be hard to explain to anyone else.

My father was fucking her very roughly, and in moments he started to cum. It wasn't long after my mother did. But, at the last moment, he pulled his cock out of her and directed it down, and he ejaculated long streams of white cum onto my cock and balls. A lot of my own cum had already dripped from my mother's cunt and onto my penis when it first slipped out of her. When we parted, my cock was a mess with a mixture of my cum and father's cum—and it was mixed with mother's sweet pussy juice that I later learned was from her FE...Female Ejaculation.

I went in and took a hot shower and fell into bed drained and exhausted. As I went to sleep, I wished that I hadn't agreed to go to the beach with Jason and Brianna the next day. I was tired and hoped that I could at least get some sleep on the sand. If it weren't for the chance to see Brianna and possibly Cindy in their bikinis, I would have canceled.

## Chapter 04

The day was already warm when Jason and Brianna picked me up a little after eight in the morning. On our way to the beach, we drove over and picked Cindy up at her house. When we got to the beach, I was surprised to see that it was already getting a little crowded with other beachgoers. We set up at our regular spot on the beach, and, I have to tell you, watching Brianna and Cindy as they spread the towels and blanket on the sand and then putting suntan lotion on their young bodies was a guaranteed hard-on getter for me! Cindy's tits were definitely overflowing the material of her bikini top, and Brianna was wearing a small bikini bottom that didn't match the top. It showed the distinct impression of her camel toe when she turned a certain way.

I was glad that Cindy joined us, she and Jason were hitting it off, and the four of us really had a great time. Brianna was reading a paperback. I managed to fall asleep for a very short nap only to be interrupted by Jason purposely dripping water on me after he and Cindy had returned from a swim in the surf.

A little later in the day, I was reading; the girls were playing in the waves that came up to about their waists and occasionally a little higher. Jason kept his eyes on the girls, especially Cindy, and he said, "Hey man, you're missing a great tittie-show...look at those things bounce." I looked at Cindy, and Jason was right; each time she'd jump over a low wave, her tits bounced erotically on her chest even with her bikini top holding them tightly in place. I also wondered if the water made Brianna's camel toe any more evident. I hoped it did.

"Whew, I'd love to slide my dick between those nice warm tits and tittie-fuck her," Jason quietly said as he continued to watch Cindy. "You ever do that?"

His question really surprised me. "Um, no—not yet." I answered.

"I did, once; I came all over her throat and chin—it was incredibly hot."

"Who?" I asked. I knew all of his past girlfriends, and I thought he'd told me about all of their sexual escapades, especially one like that.

He hesitated as if he was sorry he'd said anything. "It was um...Megan...my ex-girlfriend," he said unconvincingly.

"Megan?"

I didn't believe him. Jason could never keep something like that a secret for very long. Besides, I was pretty sure that Megan just didn't have tits large enough to do that with. I was about to press the point further, but the girls were just returning from the water. I immediately noticed the impressions of Brianna's nipples in the fabric of her bikini top, and I wondered what it would be like to tittie-fuck her—then I thought about tittie-fucking my mother, and I knew that all I had to do was ask. Undoubtedly she'd agree as a part of my sex education.

Later I went down to the water to take a swim, and after a few minutes, Brianna joined me. We stood in the low surf, talked, and just kind of hung out together. A couple of times, she almost lost her balance as we jumped some of the smaller waves. After one particularly strong wave, she held my hand to help steady herself. Under the thin material of her bikini, her camel toe was very pronounced, and we went deeper into the surf, mainly to hide my throbbing hard-on. A little time later, a large and completely unexpected wave suddenly knocked both Brianna and me off our feet, and we clung together as we scrambled to stand back up. Our arms were around each other. Her tits were pressing against my chest, and she laughed and sputtered water out of her mouth. A second and even more powerful wave hit us again knocked us down. As we were tossed in the wet, strong turmoil, several times, her hand brushed against my hard cock that was trapped in my bathing suit. We both were laughing and still holding each other as we managed to finally stand in the chest-deep water. "Oh, my god," she laughed. The wave had pushed her bikini top up to her neck and completely exposing her beautiful naked breast. I was glad that we were far out enough in the surf that no one on the beach seemed to notice. "I wish I could just leave my top off, it feels so free and natural but," she paused. "Sometimes everybody's so uptight about sex," she said wistfully. She pressed her naked breast against my chest for a moment as we just looked at each other. I was sure she could feel my hard-on against her body. She put the top back on and smiled at me with a mischievous look in her eyes as she reached back to re-tie the bikini strings.

"It probably doesn't help that this is the time of the month that I get so horny," she said with a laugh.

"I'm always horny," I said. Immediately wishing I hadn't said it. It sounded dumb. Brianna laughed as we waded through the water toward the shallow surf near the beach. When we were out of the water, she glanced at me and said with a smile, "You're always horny? You're just like Jason, at least we got a good sex education, so that helps," she laughed as she turned. Her statement, especially the words sex education, really jolted me! What did she mean by that? Is there even the slightest chance that she knows what my parents and I are doing? Why would she say that? I wondered. I just stood there looking at her as she walked toward our blankets. Jason and Cindy were watching us while returning, so I tried to act natural. At least my hard-on had gone down and wasn't so noticeable.

The rest of the afternoon, we all had a good time in the water and on the sand, and as it worked out, I was never alone with Brianna again the rest of the day. We left the beach late in the afternoon and stopped for burgers on our way home. I finally got to the house at about eight p.m., just as it was getting dark. My mother and father were in the spa on the patio, naked, and I waved at them before going to my room and getting undressed. I needed a shower to rinse the sand and sunscreen off of my body before joining them in the spa. As I stood under the shower, the hot water felt good running over my naked body. I still couldn't shake Brianna's earlier remark about sex education. Maybe it wasn't just the words that bothered me; maybe it was the way she said it? I had the feeling that somehow she knew what was happening between my parents and me, but that couldn't be possible, I kept telling myself.

I closed my eyes and thought about Brianna lying on a bed, her hands pressing her luscious breasts together as I was straddling her chest and stroking the warm flesh between her naked breasts with my cock. I could almost hear her voice softly urging me on, anxious for me to ejaculate streams of cum on her neck and chin when I came on her. My imagination gently shifted back and forth between Brianna and my mother as my partners in the erotic act.

After my shower, I left my room to join my parents in the spa. Just the thought of what would undoubtedly happen made my cock tingle and throb as it began to get erect. As I passed by my parents' bedroom, I saw my father putting the small flash drive back on his bedside table. My curiosity was very strong, and I was very curious about what was on it, but I continued to the spa on the patio.

As I started to get into the spa, I caught mother looking at my cock before I slipped into the warm water. I sat next to her, and immediately I felt her hand on my thigh close to my cock. I reciprocated by placing my hand high on her thigh, the tip of my little finger just above her clitoris. After several minutes my father came back and joined us. His cock was extremely hard, and he seemed proud of it as he took his time getting into the spa.

"Mmmm, that'll feel good a later on," mother giggled as she looked at my father. "Very nice," she added.

"All for you my darling," he said as he stroked it, then added, "wherever you want me to put it," He sat in the spa directly opposite mother and me. Mother asked me how the beach was, and the three of us chatted about it for a while. A couple of times, my mother asked me some questions about Brianna. Although she's never said anything directly, I began to think that she might suspect how I feel about Brianna. The fact that Brianna's my cousin was even more embarrassing.

Under the water, Mother was stroking my cock in a very gentle way by pulling my foreskin all the way over my cock-head before pulling it all the way down again. My little finger had parted her labia at her clitoris, and I was lightly rolling it from side to side. Before long, my father moved over and sat on the other side of my mother. I felt his hand press against mine as he stuck two fingers into her vagina and started to finger-fuck her. Mother took father's cock in her other hand, and she was playing with both of our cocks as we sat beside her in the spa. Our dual assault on her cunt made her spread her thighs apart as far as she could, giving the two important men in her life more access to her sexual treasures.

Mother was clearly enjoying the attention father, and I was giving her.

"Oh god, you both are turning me on so much," she said softly. "Let's go to bed where we can be more comfortable." The three of us got out of the spa and dried off before going into their bedroom. Father and I both had raging hard-ons, which didn't escape my mother's attention as she lay down on the bed. I was so horny I could hardly wait until I could get between her legs and fuck her, but I sensed that this time my father would be the one to fuck her first as I watched.

Mother turned on her left side and pulled her right leg, the one on top, all the way up toward her body. In this position, her pussy and anus were completely available to enjoy. She was

caressing her naked breasts, and her breathing was rapid. She moaned as my father positioned himself above her. His eyes seemed locked-on on her cunt. He was slowly stroking his cock as he straddled my mother's right thigh and moved closer to her cunt. It seemed as if, for the moment at least, he wasn't sure which of her holes to fuck. He began teasing my mother's swollen clit with the engorged tip of his penis. Each time it passed over her clit, it sent an erotic shiver through her sensitive, anxious body. Before long, he reached over and opened the drawer of his bedside table and pulled out a large tube of KY lubricant. I saw the flash drive in the drawer before he closed it, and it rekindled my curiosity. Turning back to my mother, he directed the head of his cock back slightly and began rubbing it on my mother's anus. He stopped for a moment and handed me the tube of KY and, with a deep, lust-filled voice, said, "Get your mother ready for me."

I knew what he meant, and as he continued teasing her exposed clit with his hard cock, I squeezed a glob of the clear lubricant directly on mother's tight anus. I worked the lubricant around my mother's anus with my fingers— I took my time getting her ready. I couldn't believe how turned on I was, not to mention that my precum was actually dripping slowly out of the end of my cock. I was totally possessed by my desire and pure lust for what was happening at the moment.

"Let me make it easier for you men," Mother said as she rolled over on the bed and got on her hands and knees, positioning herself directly in front of her husband's hard dick.

I squeezed another large glob of KY directly on her hole to work it inside her. With two of my fingers, I concentrated on her anus before I pressed them past her tight anal ring and easily slipped inside. I worked as much of the KY onto her tight hole as I could, and I could feel her muscles relaxing. In moments she was ready to be fucked. I spread the remaining KY that was still on my fingers on the head of my father's cock-it just seemed like the normal thing to do...so I did it. I could tell he enjoyed it even though he kept watching me getting my mother's anus ready for his intimate anal assault.

"Direct me in, son," my father said. I took his hard penis in my hand and directed the swollen head against her puckered hole. I held it steady as my father began to gently push his head against my mother's anus until it finally yielded. I watched as his swollen, purple head disappeared inside her. She let out a loud cry as my father's cock continued to fill her hole. "Oh fuck baby that feels so good," my mother groaned. Once father's cock was

completely inside her, he hesitated before withdrawing it almost completely out of her. In moments he began a steady rhythm as he fucked her ass. Mother pushed her hips back each time his cock filled her. The room was filled with her soft moans and mother's occasional whimpering. I couldn't get over how erotic her naked body looked.

Soon the whole room was filled with the sounds and the vision of intense anal sex—of my father roughly fucking my mother in the ass. I was holding, caressing, and stroking my cock as I watched them, knowing that in moments I was next.

Mother's tits, hanging from her chest, bounced violently each time father rammed his hard cock into her hole. Her moaning was constant as the pleasure seemed to spill out of her. Father was beginning to moan in a deep voice that sounded like a growl. Several minutes passed as they fucked, and I simply watched them.

"Donna, I'm getting closer, do you want me to cum in your ass or pull it out and cum on your back?" Father groaned to her.

"Don't pull it out! Fill my ass with your hot cum...I know I'll cum when you do...just empty your big balls and fill me with your hot cum...fill me so our son watches us!"

Mother reached out and took my hand in hers, held it tightly, and squeezed it several times as her pleasure ran through her. Their tempo became frantic as their naked bodies slapped together in delicious, mind-numbing lust. Father was fucking mother hard, and she couldn't seem to get enough.

"Fuck Donna, fuck Donna," father said loudly. "I'm about to cum!"

"Yes, cum in me...fill me!" She demanded.

"Here it comes! FUCK DONNA I'M CUMMING IN YOUR ASS...NOW!" His face was contorted with the sweet intensity of his orgasm and powerful ejaculation. "Oh fuck Donna...fuck," he moaned.

Mother emitted a sharp cry as her body began to shudder, "I'M CUMING TOO! Fuck me! Fuck me! Oh fuck! I can feel your cum baby!" Mother held her breath for a moment, her body shuddering before moaning and crying out, "Yes, oh fuck me Baby!"

Mother's words turned to moans as my father continued to pump her ass full of his cum.

Granted, my sex education was still all very new, but I've never seen my father cum this hard before. Even as they slowed, each following pulse of his cock made his body jolt and moan softly.

My parents both came hard, and their bodies seemed to recover more slowly than usual. I was so incredibly horny I could hardly wait to fuck mother. My father slowly pulled his cock out of my mother's vagina, and I'll never forget the sight of his white cum as it slowly seeped from my mother's well-stretched and well-fucked anus. Father moved to the side of mother on the bed as I took his place behind her upturned bright red ass. Spread her cheeks with my hands and saw another large glob of cum starting to ooze out of her anus. Father surprised me when he reached over and took my cock in his hand and placed the head of my cock against mother's cum filled opening and said, "Push yourself inside your mother and fuck her. She's close and it won't take much to make her cum again." I did as he said, and I watched as my cock disappeared into her body, filling her completely. Mother moaned loudly as my cock filled her anus, and I began to fuck her. I'd never had anal sex with a woman before, and I was surprised at how tight her anus felt around my cock even though, between the KY gel and father's cum, there was plenty of lubrication.

Father got up from the bed and went into the bathroom, leaving mother and me alone for a moment. I reached around her body with my right hand and held her right breast as I kept pumping my cock into her ass. I lost track of time. "Damn I whispered!"

"What's the matter baby?" She asked.

"Mom, I don't know how much longer I can hold it back. I'm so close," I groaned. "I'm about to cum! I don't think I can hold it back any longer. I want it to last but I can't." I was angry at myself that I couldn't last longer but fucking my mother's naked body as she knelt on her hands and knees on the bed before me.

"Let it come baby," she moaned. "Let it cum inside me...I want every drop of your cum inside me! Just like your father. Fuck my ass baby, fuck me...fuck your mother."

Her words were all that it took for me to lose complete control. I started fucking her as hard as I could, and after only a few strokes, my orgasm slammed into me. I could feel my cum rushing up from my balls and out my penis and into her beautiful anus. I'd never felt anything like it before—it was different from vaginal sex. The intense feeling of my orgasm rolled through me as I pumped my cum into my mother's anus.

My father had come out of the bathroom and was standing beside the bed, watching us.

We stayed in the same position as our orgasms subsided, enjoying what we'd just shared. I felt my cock softening and, even though I wasn't ready to pull it out of her anus, there was little I could do; it was coming out. When my cock slipped free of her hole, it was followed by a large white stream of cum that ran over her cunt lips and onto the bed. Father immediately reached for the cum and, with his fingers, spread it all over my mother's stretched anus and cunt. He even spread what was left on my soft cock. I didn't care; it felt good!

Mother's pussy lips and anus were smeared with cum as she got off the bed. "Come take a shower with me," she said as she held out her hand. I went into the shower stall with her; the warm water felt good as it cascaded over our bodies as we washed each other off. Mother soaped my cock and balls and anus, washing the lube and cum off of me. When it was my turn, I returned the favor and lathered her body from her tits to her cunt. I admit I washed her pussy a little longer than necessary. I turned her around and washed the cum off of her well-fucked anus. The fact that we were taking a shower together made me hard again, not to mention the incredible feeling of her feminine hands as she handled my penis.

After we were clean, we embraced and kissed each other passionately. I could feel her naked breasts pressing against my chest as our tongues dueled erotically. Her breath was warm and feminine. It was very obvious that my mother was still horny and wanted more sex. "I want to look deep into your beautiful eyes as you fuck me. I want to look deep into your eyes as my vagina holds your cock as if it will never let it go," she whispered. "I want to feel your cum deep inside me...warming me from the inside." Mother took my cock and gently rubbed the head against her sensitive clitoris as she let out a low moan. We stood under the shower for a while, still embracing as we enjoyed the touch and desire of each other's bodies.

When we finally got out of the shower, we toweled ourselves off, and before leaving the bathroom, mother dropped to her knees and took my cock in her mouth, and began to suck it. It was only about half-hard but quickly hardened when surrounded by her warm mouth and lips. I watched as she repeatedly took my full length into her mouth and throat. Her dark, wet hair hung down in tangled strands that covered most of her face.

I could feel my orgasm starting to stir as her tongue worked on the sensitive underside of my cock. Suddenly she let my cock slip from her mouth as she stood up, and we kissed passionately once again. When we broke off our kiss, she looked into my eyes and said, "Let's go back in the bedroom so we can fuck slowly, and with passion. I want to take the time to hold you and feel you deep inside me as we fuck," she paused. "We can make love and share ourselves with each other as if it's the only thing that matters in the world."

As I followed her into the bedroom, I couldn't get over how erotic her naked body looked as she walked before me. It was so easy for me to forget that she was my mother - most of all, she is a woman with her femininity, full of life, and full of needs - strong sexual needs.

For some reason, I noticed that the skin across her shoulders and down her back looked smooth, soft, and inviting to touch, just like Brianna's.

Father was in the spa, so it was just the two of us in the bedroom. We stopped next to the bed and embraced, looking into each other's eyes between our passionate kisses, our naked bodies pressed tightly together, and the room seemed to be filled with an erotic passion to possess each other. I eased her down on the bed where she lay on her back. She looked up at me with a look of vulnerability and desire. I positioned myself on my hands and knees above her naked body. The head of my hard cock was resting on her warm pussy lips, and, for the moment, I made no attempt to push my cock into her vagina—her eyes told me that there was plenty of time. I could feel her warm breath on my chest, and I leaned down and took one of her hard nipples into my lips and began to suck on it. I purposely made soft sucking sounds, which caused her body to shudder in response. As I continued to suck on her nipples, her breath began to become more erratic.

She wrapped her arms around my back and whispered into my ear, "Fuck me baby, put yourself inside me slowly; let me feel every inch of your cock inside me before we start to fuck."

I did as she asked, and I slowly started to push my penis into her vagina. I stopped for a moment a couple of times before I was completely inside her. It is the moment of possession, the moment when people are the most vulnerable with another human being, and thus, should be one of the most intimate moments that two people can share.

I slowly began to fuck mother with long gentle strokes. There was no hurry. I would withdraw until nothing but the swollen head of my cock was inside her. Then, I'd slowly travel up the full length of her vagina until my scrotum and balls prevented me from going any deeper. We fucked slowly and sensuously, and at one point, mother looked at me and smiled as she straightened some of my hair on my forehead with her fingers. Something she'd done for as long as I could remember.

I lost track of time. All that mattered was that a very feminine woman and I were enjoying each other, and I never wanted it to end. We took our time. For the longest time, we simply didn't hurry. Even though we were fucking at a slower pace, I have to admit that I still had to pace myself to keep from cuming too soon. We'd fuck slowly for a few minutes at a time before we'd stop and kiss or, I'd play with—or suck on her tits. We talked about sex, not just the sex we were sharing at that moment. Mother showed no inhibitions about fucking her son; to the contrary, it aroused her to an intense level of pleasure.

We fucked like that for over an hour, taking our time to enjoy each other. At some point, we'd slowly begun to fuck with more urgency, a little at a time. Mother kept her eyes on mine as our tempo picked up. Soon I was fucking her with hard strokes that pounded her warm cunt, and she met every one of my strokes by thrusting her hips back at me. I knew that the powerful feeling that was building inside both of us would demand a release as if it had a life of its own. And it would be very soon.

"Fuck me my baby...oh, you're so big and hard and it feels so good...fuck me!" She whispered as her face contorted from her pleasure.

"Fuck me my beautiful, handsome man!"

"Baby, does it feel good to fuck me? To fuck your mother?" She moaned. "Fuck me, baby, I'm so close." I felt her body stiffen as she cried out. "OH MY GOD BABY...I'M CUMING—I'M CUMING!"

Mother's body jolted several times violently as her orgasm peaked inside her body, and I fucked her as hard and fast as I could. Within a few strokes, my orgasm slammed into me. My penis felt as if it had exploded inside her. I could feel my cum as it traveled up my cock and spurted into the depths of her vagina, even though it wasn't nearly as much as the first ejaculation I gave her.

Mother was thrashing beneath me as her orgasm flooded through her naked body. Her arms wrapped around me as if— she was trying to pull me completely inside her. Her moaning gently turned into a quiet sobbing as tears ran from the corners of her eyes and down her cheek, and I simply held her.

"Are you alright?" I finally whispered.

"Yes, it's just so beautiful and...so special. I can't explain it. I don't know why I'm crying, I can't help it. I'm not sad," she paused. "I'm just overwhelmed by what we just shared and how beautiful it was. These are tears of deep joy...not sorrow."

It took a little time for us to come down from our orgasms, and my mother's body was still very sensitive. After her orgasm, my mother continued to have several smaller ones as we lay in bed holding each other. I very gently sucked on one of her nipples, which immediately brought on a smaller, but intense orgasm in her. She had another one when my softening cock slipped out of her cum-filled vagina. She was that sensitive and aroused.

I felt as if every ounce of energy had left my body with my ejaculation, and it felt good to simply lie in bed with her, sharing the tender moments right after our shared orgasms.

A little later, father came into the bedroom and sat on the edge of the bed with us. His hand brushed roughly against my cock as he reached for mother's wet cunt. His fingers parted her lips, and a large glob of my cum was released and began to run down over mother's pussy toward her anus. With his fingers, he collected as much as he could, and he began to spread it over his hard cock. I got up from the bed to give them more room, and I stood next to the bed watching as father lay down on his back, his cock standing straight up. Mother quickly moved over and straddled his hips so that her cunt was directly above his cock. With her fingers, she positioned the crimson head of his cock at the entrance of her vagina, and as she eased herself down father's cock and it disappeared into her vagina. I remember seeing that her cunt was still a bright pink color from our recent fuck.

"Nothing feels better than fucking with cum as a lubricant," father said softly.

I sat on the edge of the bed watching them fuck, and even though I was soft, I wanted to fuck mother again. The sight of her pussy riding up and down on my father's cock was incredible. It was then that something happened that really surprised me. They were fucking with a steady rhythm when

mother took my father's hand and placed it directly on my cock, and he began caressing and stroking it with his fingers as they fucked. I was surprised, but it felt good. I didn't care. There were only three of us in the room, and I trusted them, and I was sure that what happened in the room stayed in the room.

Before long, the atmosphere in the room was so sexually charged that my cock was getting hard again as my father played with it as he fucked my mother. For obvious reasons, I'd never seen my parents as turned-on as they were at that moment. Father was running his hand up and down my cock, jacking me off, and the feeling was incredible. I wasn't ready to cum so soon after my last orgasm, but I didn't care; it felt good.

Mother was fucking father faster and harder. Every time she opened her eyes, she watched father playing with my cock, and it seemed to turn her on even more. Suddenly she cried-out loudly, her body slamming against my father's body that lay beneath her as she came again. "Fuck, fuck, oh my pussy feels so good! Fuck me!" She cried out as her body jolted with pleasure. "I'm cuming...oh fuck...fuck...yes!"

"Fuck yes Donna, I'm cuming too baby!" My father groaned loudly. "Fuck Donna...here...it...comes!"

He held my cock and squeezed it firmly as he ejaculated his hot cum into mother's pussy—the same hole that I'd ejaculated into ten minutes or so before. When things slowed, without a word being spoken, he finally took his hand off my cock. I noticed that his hand had a lot of my pre-cum on it.

The three of us were exhausted, and we lay on the bed, enjoying what we'd shared together. It was then that I first realized that my parents were introducing something new to my sex education, my mother's approval and encouragement of my father's secret. The subtle signs were there all along. I just never recognized them before.

I couldn't shake the feeling that there was more, maybe a lot more, that they might be hiding, and the answers might be on the flash drive in father's drawer.

# Chapter 05

There is no doubt that the relationship between my parents has changed. With my mother, most of the time, I'd see her in a normal, nonsexual mother-son relationship. Sometimes, especially when we were alone together, things between us were perfectly normal—as if we'd never crossed the taboo line. Other times, especially at night, I'd see her as an erotic, highly sexual woman, a woman whose slightest look was capable of stirring deep arousal and desire within me.

It took me a while to realize that our relationship started to change. It changed the first time I pushed my hard cock into her sweet, wet vagina, and we started to fuck. I can't help but feel that when I finally ejaculated inside her that first time, our relationship was different (in a very good way).

The relationship between my father and I also changed. He's a masculine man and, like my mother, loves sex. As my sex education progressed, obviously, I came to see a side of him—or desire that he, my mother, and only a few other people knew about. Our relationship quickly matured away from the typical father/son relationship, and we moved to an equal man to man relationship. A lot of things became more open, and I know that I learned and matured a lot. My father always got very aroused, watching my mother having sex. I liked watching and being with them when they fuck. It's their most vulnerable moments that I find very erotic When they fuck there's a strong sexual urgency between them that would fill the room. Their moans and cries of passion and vulgar sex talk mixed with the sound of their flesh slapping loudly together until they would cum together was incredible.

I'd never really realized it before, but mother seemed to always be aroused. It's something that simmers just below the surface in her. Once her sexual desires are released, she becomes insatiable until it's satisfied; and much of the time, it took at least two men, my father and I, to completely satisfy her.

Our family's dynamics had changed too. The three of us immediately shed a lot of our inhibitions. Nudity was simply no big deal. While in the house, the spa, or in the back garden, we rarely wore clothes anymore. Often my parents would fuck in the spa or in the den, or anywhere in the house. If they fucked in their bedroom, they never closed the door, and many times

I'd walk in and watch them, sometimes jacking off as I did. In fact, my mother and I did the same in my bedroom so my father could watch us fuck. They both enjoyed masturbation and seemed to especially enjoy watching me as I jack-off, so I usually leave my bedroom door open in case they wanted to watch.

Several days after my father and I fucked mother in the ass, my parents were in the spa, and I took advantage of the situation to go into their bedroom specifically to see if the flash drive was still on my father's bedside table. I felt odd sneaking in like that, but I was curious. When I opened the drawer, the flash drive was gone. I felt a mixture of disappointment as well as relief.

A little later that same evening, I joined them in the spa, and after some time had passed, I simply asked,

"What's on the flash drive that you keep in the drawer next to your bed?"

Both of them were momentarily stunned at my question, and they looked at each other.

"How do you know about that?" My father asked. "Did you look at it?"

"No," I answered. "I knew you kept it in the drawer but I didn't look at it."

It was obvious that both my parents were unsettled by my question, and they were quiet for a long moment.

Mother took a deep breath and said, "It has lot of secrets on it...family secrets...our families' secrets. We've always planned on sharing it with you at a time when it seemed right. But, I don't know, we were just waiting for the right time to explain some things to you."

"What do you mean secrets? What kind of secrets?" I said, unsure of what she meant. "With what we've been doing," I paused a moment. "My sex education I mean...that's a pretty big secret, what could be bigger than that?"

"The flash drive contains a lot of old and new photo and video files that we've kept for years," my father said. "Some of the photos are old and were taken even before your mother and I got married. I've been putting them on the flash drive for several years now."

"So? I mean, considering what we've been doing, having so much sex. What's the big deal about that?

Are there photos of the three of us having sex?"

"Not yet," my father said. "But we hope there will be," My father said. "We'd only do it if you agreed."

"Sure, I'd like that," I said honestly. The idea of being able to watch myself as I had sex with my parents, especially fucking my mother, really turned me on.

The three of us were quiet for a moment, and I was still a little confused by my parent's uneasiness over the flash drive.

Mother looked directly at me and said, "It's not just some random photos and videos, it's a lot more. Our family has always been very close. Next to you and your father, my sister Carol and her family are the closest people in my life. We've always been that way."

"As you obviously know, your mother and I are very sexual people," my father added. "We've always kept it hidden from you but now that you're of age we wanted to be honest with you by opening our sex lives and secrets with you. As your mother said, there are a lot of secrets on the flash drives."

"What kind of secrets?" I wasn't sure what he meant, and I glanced at my mother.

Let's get out of the spa and go into the den where we can be more comfortable, and we can talk," she said as she stood up as the warm water cascaded off her body.

As we dried off, the three of us didn't say anything. But my father had a raging hard on that I was sure needed to be satisfied several times. My father used his towel to dry my back, and his right hand quickly went to my cock, and he caressed it. I didn't say anything; I just enjoyed it. We followed mother into the den, and I sat in an overstuffed chair directly across from the sofa. They sat side by side, facing me, and my father was caressing his hard cock as we got settled. Mother sat with her legs slightly spread so that I could clearly see her lovely pink pussy. She wanted me to see it, and I knew that she wanted me to fuck it before the night was over. She was very turned on. Occasionally her hand would gently come to rest on her pussy, and she would finger her clitoris with the lightest touch before taking her hand away. Her pussy lips were a deep rose color that stood-out in contrast with the whiteness of her naked thighs.

"There are a couple more flash drives than the one you saw in my bedside table my father said. We've been adding things to them for several years."

"What sort of things?" I asked.

"It started with old photos of your mother and I having sex...even before we were married. As time went on we added homemade sex videos, things like that," He said. "We now have a large collection of family erotica. "

"So they're pictures and DVDs of you and mother having sex," I asked.

"Uh huh," he said, then he paused. "But there's a lot more too."

"Let me start at the beginning," mother said. She took a slow, deep breath as she looked at me. "As you know, your aunt Carol and I had a rough childhood, we got kicked around a lot, there was just a lot of uncertainty in our lives. We came to realize that we could only depend on each other. I guess you'd say that college was difficult for us because we just had a hard time trusting other people. We were in our early twenties and pretty naive. The first time Carol and I had sex was when we were in college; obviously it was a well-kept secret. We depended on each other and somehow having sex with each other seemed normal and good. We didn't talk about it much, it just happened. Every time we had sex was better than the time before. We continued to have sex even after we both were married. It wasn't until your father and I had been married for about a year before I admitted it to him. As usual he was very understanding."

"Understanding is not quite the word for it," he said with a soft chuckle. "I loved it. Your mother and I are very sexual people. Before we met we both were sexually active and one of the things that made our marriage so strong is that we shared and enjoyed the same things about sex."

"Do you still have sex with Aunt Carol?" I asked.

"Yes," she admitted.

"Is that what's on the flash drive?"

"Well...yes," she smiled.

"There's a lot more on the flash drive than just that," my father said. "Like your mother said, we love sex. And for as long as we've been married, we've expanded the boundaries of our sex life. We had a very open marriage; sex with other people is what I mean. All most all were couples like us. We met them at parties." He hesitated a moment as his hand moved down and started gently caressing his erect cock. "I've taken a lot of

pictures and videos over the years...that's what's on the flash drives, years of adult sex." He paused as if he was slightly unsure of how to say what he said next. "They also contain a lot of family sex...we're not the only ones in our family who loves sex."

I was quiet for a moment; my mind was still wondering what Brianna or Jason would think if they knew about the flash drives and that our mothers had sex with each other? I was so focused on the question that I hadn't realized that I started caressing my cock as well, but I didn't care; it felt good.

"Are you okay with what we're telling you?" My mother asked.

"Yes." I assured her.

"Sex is an important part of life for some of the adults in our families, and those flash drives hold many secrets," mother said. "Those flash drives go back many years," she paused for a moment as if she was thinking about what she was about to say. Things really got started in a big way when your father took a lot of photos of your Aunt Stacy and her husband Greg right after they were married. The four of us would get together on Saturday nights for sex. Greg had a pretty average cock, not as big as yours or your father's, but he really knew how to use it. After they moved to Florida, we didn't see as much of them as we would have liked."

"We agreed that when you were old enough and we told you about our secrets it would be best to go slow, we know it's a lot to handle," my mother smiled at me as she placed her right hand over her pussy and rubbed it slightly. Her middle finger parted her pussy lips, and I watched as her finger disappeared into her vagina for a few seconds before she pulled it out again and concentrated on her clit.

"There are a lot of old photographs, Polaroid's and a few old 8mm movie that your grandfather took a long time ago of your grandmother being fucked by five men in a motel room on her thirty-fifth birthday. There are old black and white photos of your grandparents having sex with some of their old friends and of course, at some of our family adult parties from a long time ago. My parents were swingers many years ago and I never even suspected it, at least not until I got older."

"Did you have sex with grandmother?" I boldly asked him.

My father chuckled and answered, "Yes, a lot—it started right after I met your mother. It's one of the reasons we wanted to give you our version of a sex education, we both were pretty anxious to have you start enjoying sex with your mother. When

we were all adults my brothers and I fucked our mother a lot and dad has fucked all of our wives." "Did he fuck you?" I asked my mother. She smiled and nodded as she said, "Yes, a lot. He fucked me at almost every party we went to. I think I was his favorite. He had a lot of stamina. He was very good at it, especially performing oral sex. He loved to clean your grandmother up when she had sex with other men and was full of cum."

"We love sex and tried to never judge what other people did in sexually, everyone's different but no one ever had to do anything they didn't feel comfortable doing, especially about family sex."

I was a little hesitant, but I finally asked the obvious question. "Do Brianna and Jason know about the flash drives? Do they know that you and their mother have sex?" I asked as I looked at my mother.

"Yes," she answered. "Carol and your uncle Ray started Jason and Brianna's sex education almost a year ago. It's been Carol's idea for years, we all talked about it a lot over the years and your father and I liked the idea for several obvious reasons."

I was stunned by the thought of Brianna and Jason fucking each other and fucking their parents, and I almost came at just the thought as I sat in the chair. I could hardly think. My hand was drenched with precum, and I stopped rubbing myself, and I kept glancing at my mother's cunt.

"My pussy is so wet and I'm so horny...do you like seeing my cunt baby? Do you like to see the wet hole where you've already left so much of your cum?" She was so turned on that I could see the wetness that was seeping out of her vagina.

"Let me help you get off Donna," my father said as he turned toward her. I watched as his hand went directly to her cunt. He rubbed her clit for several minutes before he spread her pussy lips and pushed two fingers into her hole, and started finger-fucking her. She immediately began to moan as the sloshing sound of her wet cunt filled the room. I could see the muscles on her abdomen jolting spasmodically as father's fingers fucked her hard and deeply.

My mind was still on the thought of Brianna getting fucked by Jason, her father Ray, maybe even some of my uncles. And I also wondered if maybe my father had already fucked her.

Just then, mother let out a high-pitched whine as a very fast orgasm exploded inside her. "Fuck! Oh fuck, fuck, fuck!" she

cried out. I glanced down and saw my father's cock spurting streams of his cum on mother's thigh as she squeezed and jerked his cock roughly. I was that close to cuming too. I didn't dare even touch my super sensitive cock for fear that it would ejaculate immediately on its own. I wanted to hold back my orgasm, saving my first cum for the dark, warm depths of my mother's vagina.

Father slowed his fingering of mother's pussy before he moved back on the sofa and bent forward and began licking his cum off of her thigh. Mother held her eyes closed and ran her fingers through his hair as she enjoyed the moment of deep intimacy with her husband.

When she opened her eyes, she looked directly at me and asked again, "I know I've asked you this before but I'll ask again, are you okay with everything we've been telling you about our family secrets? We want you to see everything on the flash drives but we wanted to, sort of, prepare you a little. It's quite a secret our family holds."

"Yes, I'm fine with it," I answered honestly."

"Good, because there's more,"

We just looked at each other as father finished licking up his cum; it was an incredibly erotic sight. I could see a white drop of cum that was still dripping out of the end of his cock. I don't know why but I had the strongest urge to get up from my chair, move over and suck the remaining cum out of his cock, but I didn't move.

When he pulled his fingers out of my mother's stretched vagina, the opening was slow to close completely, and for a moment, I could see the tunnel of darkness that was inside her vagina. I was fighting to keep from cuming, and the sight of her hole was almost more than I could handle. I was surprised when she looked at me and said, "Are you about to cum?"

"Yes," I nodded.

"Cum inside me baby...come over here, fuck me and leave your cum inside me."

I moved over toward the sofa as she pulled her knees up toward her chest spreading her legs even wider. I quickly got between her legs, knowing I would cum at any moment. I slipped the swollen head of my cock into her hole, and after only a few strokes, I felt my cock beginning to spew my cum into my mother's cunt. "I'm...sorry," I moaned, "I can't stop it

mother...I'm cuming! Oh fuck mother, I'm cuming! Fuck!" I pounded her warm pussy as hard as I could, but I was too late. I was already cuming.

Mother kept whispering," Yes baby, fuck your mother...leave your cum inside me...fuck me! Cum in me!" Several moments afterward, my father got off of the sofa and left the room as my mother, and I remained locked in our sexual embrace. My penis was still held inside her vagina. It was occasionally pulsing in an attempt to empty every bit of my cum inside her. We stayed on the sofa like that—simply holding each other—sharing the most wonderful emotional feelings between a mother and a son after having sex with each other—even if the sex was only for a very few moments. It was obvious to me that I'd managed to empty every drop of cum into my mother's vagina just then but, I also knew that very soon I'd be able to cum again.

My mind was reeling with the things that my parents had been telling me. My intense curiosity about how Brianna might participate in family sex was foremost in my mind. 'My God,' I thought, what she must look like lying on a bed with her perfect legs spread apart as some man in our family fucks her...I could only imagine.

I got off my mother's body and sat back on the sofa next to her as my father came back into the room. He sat next to me on the sofa. He glanced at mother and asked, did you tell him about—"

"No, I was just about to when you came back."

"Tell me what?" I asked.

"I'll tell him," he said cheerfully. His cock was hard again, and he started rubbing himself as he said, "Like your mother and I have been telling you, there's a lot on those flash drives. Mostly unrestricted family sex...everyone who participated did what they liked and, as a family, we understood and were fine with it. I know you're not aware of it but," he paused a moment before saying, "Sometimes I really like sucking a cock and having sex with another man." He paused as he put his hand on my cock and wrapped his fingers around my sticky shaft—sticky from mother and my recent fuck juices. There's a lot of video of your uncle Ray and I; your uncle Tyler and your uncle Jeff and I having man-to-man sex as well as other family members engaged in sex." He paused again. "I was in my twenties when your grandfather sucked my cock for the first time...I still remember everything that led up to it. I was over at their house helping them build a new fence, it was hot, and when we were done, I

took a shower in my old bathroom. I was about to get out of the shower when your grandfather came into the bathroom. He was nude, and without saying anything, he opened the shower door and got in with me. What surprised me the most was that he had a large cock, and it was already very hard. I didn't do or say anything, I just stood there, and he started playing with my cock. He finally asked me if I'd ever had another man suck my cock, and I honestly answered, "No." He just smiled at me and got on his knees in front of me, and started sucking my cock in the shower. I couldn't get over how good it felt, he was a very good cocksucker, and it seemed like it took a long time before I finally came. When I did cum it was really a hard one, and he swallowed every drop of my cum. I'd never known that I could have such a powerful orgasm. I was a little surprised that my knees held me up when I finally came.

"When we got out of the shower, I remember that your grandmother had been standing at the bathroom door the whole time watching your grandfather suck my cock. She had a thin cotton dress on that showed that she was naked underneath. She still had a good looking body for a woman her age, and she came right out and asked me if I enjoyed what had happened, and I told her the truth—that I loved it. Your grandfather and I were toweling off when your grandmother slipped her dress off over her shoulders and stood next to me completely naked and playfully asked, 'do you have enough cum left to fuck me too?'

I wasn't sure if I did at that moment, but it didn't matter. The three of us had our first evening of incredible sex. During that first time, they told me all about their years-long experiences as swingers, and they admitted to me for the first time that they were both bisexuals. It was a hell of an evening. It was also the first time that I sucked a cock and swallowed cum." He paused before adding, "That evening unlocked something inside me, and ever since, I've always loved the taste, the smell, and the silky texture of cum in my mouth, in my ass, and especially when it's dripping from your mother's pussy. After that first time, every time I went over to their house, it seemed that we'd end up in bed and had sex just like we're doing with you."

My father is very masculine, and I was shocked by what he admitted, yet at the same time, the thought of him having man-to-man sex, sucking on a hard cock deeply aroused me and made me very horny. There had been times that I secretly fantasized about another man shooting a load of cum in my mouth, wondering what it felt and tasted like. I never told

anyone my secret, and suddenly, after my father admitted that he, like his father, enjoyed man to man sex, it didn't seem like such a big deal.

"Before we were married, your father and I kept our secrets from each other for a while. We each wanted to tell the other about it, but we were, I don't know, afraid of what the other might think. Then one night, as we were engaged in some pretty heavy foreplay and I started to suck his cock, your father just came out and asked me what I would think if I ever saw him having sex with his father? I remember letting his cock slip from my mouth, and, I'll be honest, I was still a little unsure about sharing my secret, and I simply answered by asking him, 'what would you say if you saw me having sex with my sister?

"It was finally out, and I know we both felt so relieved that our private secrets were finally out. We talked and shared everything for what seemed like hours, holding nothing back. We both understood how important they were to each other. Your father and I enjoyed the longest foreplay we'd ever had, and afterward, we fucked for hours.

As my father sat next to me, he played with my cock, and it was slowly getting harder. His admission really aroused my mother, and she had her hand over her pussy and was gently rubbing it. "I really love to watch your father having sex...with a woman or a man...it turns me on," she said softly. "It makes me so horny. I love it when he kisses me and I can smell and taste the cum in his mouth." She was quiet for a long moment. "We could hardly wait until you were old enough to share our secrets with. We were sure that you'd understand everything and accept the fact that, as far as sex goes, we're not like other families. We're very secure in what we do and we love it."

"Have you had sex with Brianna?" I asked my father.

"No, not yet, he said with a smile, then added, "She's wasn't exactly a virgin."

I was very curious about what he meant, and at the same time, I knew the answer was on the flash drives.

"Carol and Ray started Brianna and Jason's sex education about three months ago," mother said. "It worked so well we were anxious to get started when you were old enough to join us but it had to be the right time."

My father got up and went into their bedroom, and when he returned, he was carrying a large pink vibrator that rotated back and forth and had a small bird-shaped clit stimulator on the top

of the barrel. He knelt down in front of my mother and switched it on as she spread her legs. I was captivated by the sight and sound of the vibrator slowly fucking her wet pussy. Father reached over with his right hand and started to massage my dick as he continued working on my mother's cunt. I adjusted my position and spread my thighs wide apart to give him better access to my cock and balls. I was at an incredible level of arousal; nothing mattered to me except pleasure and satisfaction. Father worked on my mother and me with complete control. His hand stroked my dick—stopping only long enough to massage my ball sack. A couple of times, his finger would brush lightly against my anus. I wasn't sure if it was accidental or not, but it didn't matter. I was driven by my powerful sexual desires that I could barely keep in check.

Mother was moaning loudly as her lower body moved to meet the vibrator each time my father pushed it into her pink fleshy hole. Soon my father was furiously fucking my mother with the pink plastic toy. Her orgasm was building, and their motion becoming more frantic as her sweet cries filled the room. "Fuck me!" She cried over and over.

For only a moment, she opened her eyes and looked at me. "Baby, hold momma's hand as I cum," she cried as her hand searched for mine. Our hands met, our fingers interwoven only moments before a flood of pleasure caused by the vibrator in father's hand slammed into her pussy and spread throughout her naked body. "Fuck! Oh my god! Fuck! My pussy's cuming! Fuck me! Fuck me and never stop," she cried loudly as her hand forcefully gripped mine. I saw a stream of clear liquid spurt forcefully from her pussy and drench my father's hand as he kept fucking her with the buzzing toy. It was the most erotic thing I'd ever seen.

When my mother's body finally relaxed somewhat, father slipped the toy from her vagina and leaned forward and buried his face in her pussy, and began licking up the fluid from her wet thighs and cunt. She actually had another small orgasm as he cleaned her up.

I'd only heard a little about FE; female ejaculation before, and when I saw it happen to mother as she came, it absolutely stunned me with the most erotic desires. It was so beautiful, sexual, and honest; it affected me deeply. Mother later told me that it didn't always happen, just certain times when she was deeply aroused; she would ejaculate the clear fluid.

The three of us stayed on the sofa in the den for a couple of hours, lounging, talking, relaxing, and enjoying the afterglow of the intense sex we had shared.

I asked a question that was still on my mind, "Are there are more secrets on the flash drive that you haven't told me about?"

Mother looked directly at me and answered, "Yes, a few. Over the years, everyone in the family was free to express themselves sexually at our family parties on often in private homes. Some even enjoy fetish play with other members of the family, and sometimes an outsider would be involved. It was never harmful, and no one was ever forced to do anything they didn't want to do. That was the strongest rule we had, and everyone obeyed it. So to answer your question simply, the answer is yes, there are other secrets on the flash drive. "However, your father and I were most concerned about how you would react to our secrets."

"To be honest, it's surprising and at the same time I really love it," I added. "I'm fine with it—it makes me feel really horny just to be a part of it."

I glanced over and saw that my father had another erection, and it was gently throbbing in his hand. He looked at his mother and said, "Donna, come over here and ride this." Mother got up from the sofa and moved over and straddled my father's waist facing toward his feet. She lowered her body down as my father directed his penis into her vagina. I watched as she slowly became impaled on his hard cock. When it was completely inside her, she rode up and down, and they fucked for several minutes until my father urged her to lie back against him. As my mother's upper body leaned back, my father's cock still stayed inside her. In this position, everything they had was fully exposed to me. As they fucked gently, my father told me to come over and eat my mother's pussy while he fucked her vagina. I got off the sofa and knelt on the floor between their legs. His wet penis was going in and out of my mother's vagina; her clitoris was completely exposed to me.

I moved forward and took mother's bright red clit in my mouth and began to lick and suck it the way she'd taught me to. With my face on her cunt, I could feel the underside of my father's cock rubbing and bumping against my chin. Mother gently held my head in place as my tongue circled and flicked at her swollen clit. Both my parents were moaning, and my nostrils were full of the thick, beautiful smell of their sex. The position was a little awkward, but incredibly erotic. I could taste mother's wetness

as it seeped out of her pussy, and I could feel my father's cock that almost felt as if it was fucking us both.

The tension and urgency of the three of us were powerful. We were in sync, giving to each other and taking from each other. The tempo of our bodies built to an unbelievable level, and suddenly, my father loudly groaned as he started to cum. He quickly pulled his wet cock out of mother's sweet, vagina and the head of his penis pushed against my lower lip as the first pulse of his cum shot out of the end of his cock and smeared on my chin. I stopped eating my mother and quickly took the head of his penis into my mouth. I was so turned on, I wanted to taste his cum, and Immediately, I felt the second, and much smaller, spurt ejaculate in my mouth as it coated my tongue with it's smooth, warm texture. I wasn't sure what to do, so I just kept sucking and milking my father's cock for anything that was left.

Mother was moaning loudly, her body almost out of control, and she quickly brought her right hand down and began slapping and rubbing her clitoris with a furious, roughness I had never seen before. In only moments the pent-up sexual tension exploded inside her as her body jolted with the most intense pleasure a woman in her position can have.

The three of us were completely exhausted and satisfied. With effort, we left the den and got into the spa. The hot water felt good against our naked skin and our well-used genitals and made us relax even more. We softly chatted as if we were somehow afraid that any loud noise would break the spell of sexual enjoyment we all shared at the moment.

"When can I see what's on the flash drive," I finally asked.

Mother looked at my father with a soft smile before turning back to me. "Anytime you want—we'll watch together."

Printed in Great Britain
by Amazon